SPELLBOUND CHRONICLES

Witch's Revenge

Written by

S.E. MAGUIRE

FastPrint Publishing

http://www.fast-print.net/bookshop

SPELLBOUND CHRONICLES: WITCH'S REVENGE
Copyright © Suzanne and Eve Maguire 2016

A catalogue record for this book is available from the British Library

ISBN 978-178456-359-2

First Published 2016 by
Fast-Print Publishing of Peterborough, England.

DEDICATION & THANKS

A special thanks to staff at Doncaster Waterstones, Paul Horsman for your patience with our endless questions, Joe for your technical advice, Leila and Emma for putting up with us for hours on end.

***

Not forgetting; Costa Coffee Janet and her lovely team who've become our friends.

***

Special thanks to our imaginative illustrator, Peter Jarvis for bringing the world, in-which the characters adventures take place, to life.

***

Many thanks to friends and family for your continued support, we couldn't have done it without you.

***

To all our fantastic readers.
The joy it brings us to know you love our stories is incredible.

***

And, to Suzanne for your bright ideas and sunny disposition each time I became crotchety.

***

We salute you one and all.

CHAPTERS

CHAPTER ONE

THE WITCHING HOUR

For several months a strange-looking female of indeterminate age and her even stranger companion had been keeping watch on 23½ Vulcan Mews where Larna Gorry, now fifteen, and her brother Aron, thirteen, lived with their mother Elizabeth. From a hidden vantage point across the road, the woman could see the siblings through their bay window and, when they went upstairs to bed, she rose silently and stared hard, willing one of them to open a window so she could enter and take possession of them. This she could only accomplish after midnight, the 'witching hour'. As it had only just turned nine o'clock she had some time to kill.

The watcher was moderately tall and slim with long black hair who cut a striking figure in purple. Her face was spoiled by a deep red, raw-looking scar which began above her left eyebrow and descended through the eyelid down her cheek, making her look waspish and spiteful. The wound obviously bothered her because she frequently traced it with the long fingers of her left hand. While her eyes were fixed on the figure of Larna closing the bedroom curtains her body began to sway back and forth. Coiled, ready to spring.

When upright, her companion only reached the woman's waist. He had a spinous tail that rattled at the end like a rattlesnake's. His skin was dull blueish-green with a scaly appearance, and he had a large concave skull with long stringy hair round a monastic tonsure crown. A pair of luminous green eyes cast twin beams from deep black holes. The creature could only be described as demonic. A chain which bound the woman's waist was loosely fastened round the creature's neck. He was anxious to be on the move.

'Patience, Selka! Not long now.' the woman cooed.

Then, out of the gloom, a man emerged, walking purposefully towards the house. He paused momentarily and looked up at the bedroom window, then glanced across the road at the two unholy beings. The woman looked horrified and began to shudder violently until her body, and that of her little partner, fragmented and dispersed into thin air. Satisfied, the man continued on his way down the road until out of sight. For the time being Larna and Aron were safe, completely unaware just how close had come to falling prey to the powers of darkness.

* * *

It had been fifteen months since Larna and Aron's last visit to Blithe Cottage in Sherwood Forest. Their maternal grandmother lived there – Neve, or Yaya as she was fondly known in the family. That had been at Easter. Now it was July of the following year and the six-week summer holidays were upon them. A couple of weeks earlier, they had been given the call to visit Sherwood again. It had been arranged for the first Saturday of the long break, the day after they broke up from school.

Their previous visit had been literally an out-of-time experience which would both haunt and fascinate the pair of them for the rest of their lives. This was when Larna and her brother had discovered that Neve, like her grandmother before her, was a white witch. They found out too that their mum, Elizabeth, hadn't inherited the gift, or curse– depending on your point of view. The two of them were left wondering if either of them had inherited their gran's powers? If so, they hadn't manifested themselves as yet.

During their first dramatic stay in the forest, Larna and Aron had travelled through a time portal and visited the Sherwood of the future. Larna often thought of the friends they had made during this amazing visit - the late great wizard, Balgaire, with his tiny companion, the gothic fairy, Violet. And of Tiblou, Balgaire's young successor, whose original contact with them in this century had begun the adventure which they would never forget. They might have attempted to return sooner had it not been for a temporary ban at the end of their previous adventure from the Grand High Council of Wizards and Witches. In their wisdom the members had decreed that, for the time being, any further contact between Tiblou in his world and the Gorrys in theirs would upset the equilibrium. All of them had to stay away from each other until they received permission which would be conveyed to the teenagers by Neve. Now, they had the 'all clear'.

In many ways, Larna and Aron had felt an enormous sense of relief at having an enforced distance between the present and future Sherwood. Their visit had been terrifying at times due to the dark forest and the evil lurking within it. Constantly in their minds was the trauma they had experienced, singly and shared, before safely returning to their own century and home. Thankfully, their mother remained in blissful ignorance of their venture into the future and from the catastrophic events which had almost cost them their lives. Neve agreed that, what their mum didn't know, couldn't hurt her. If she ever found out, she would never allow the teenagers to stay with their grandmother again.

They were keen geocache hunters, a hobby inherited from their father. This was a game in which a cache of specially hidden 'treasure' could be found by following clues downloaded from the internet. Last year he had leant Larna and Aron his GPS and, as a result, they had discovered the time portal which allowed them to visit the Sherwood of the future. This time they wouldn't need his help to locate the spot in the forest because Larna now had her own tracking device built into her smartphone, a birthday present from her parents.

However, from their previous experience, she and Aron harboured mixed feelings about the possibility of a new danger-filled visit to the future. Neither of them had discussed in depth what had happened to them, just sort of nibbled round the edges. Both were scared at how close they had come to a sticky end and chose not to talk about it for fear of frightening the other. Of the two, Aron seemed the more nervous. So Larna kept reassuring him that Mordrog the warlock was dead and his cruel servant and protégé, Edsel the Boggret, had been turned into a rat and banished forever. She knew that Aron had experienced terrible nightmares for a few months after their return home, but she'd convinced herself that he'd now fully recovered. As had she. More or less.

As soon as their mother informed them that Neve had contacted her with a suitable date for their next visit to Blithe Cottage, all Larna's anxieties had flown out of the window. As she got her things ready that Thursday evening, she tried to anticipate what breathtaking escapades they might experience during this holiday. If any. And her heart did a double beat. Would she see Cai, the shape-shifter, again?

* * *

Refreshed after a decent night's sleep, Larna and Aron washed, dressed and breakfasted in double-quick time in order to get to school early. It was the last day of the term and there was a carnival atmosphere amongst both pupils and staff. Larna looked around for Jonty, her friend since their first day at Hayfield High. They'd met at the front gate, looked at each other, felt an instant connexion and walked in together.

Larna had grown quite tall and mature during the past year and had shot past her friend. Also, her dark blonde hair had grown considerably since her last visit to Sherwood.

Over the years she and Jonty each had always been there for the other, helping each other out through the ups and down of school life. But, on the day that Larna's previous adventure had started, he'd been sent to the Headmaster's office on a wild goose chase when a terrifying spectre - an evil seething black mass - had attacked her in the school library and caused her to faint, hitting her head on the floor. It was Mr Waight, their chemistry teacher, who had found her and immediately taken control. His normally twinkling eyes looked very troubled and he had seemed greatly relieved when she slowly regained consciousness. Since then, whenever Jonty wasn't around, Mr Waight had seemed to be keeping a watchful eye on her wherever she went. She put the spectre experience down to Mordrog doing his best to keep them away from the future. But, was she right?

Leaving their backpacks in the cloakroom, Larna and Aron hurried into their respective classes for registration and then filed into the hall for the last assembly of term. This was always very long and boring with prizes and certificates to give out and a speech from the head that nobody ever listened to. At the end of this marathon, their bottoms numb from sitting for hours, the two of them filed out with their classmates to spend the day tidying out their desks, sorting their belongings and then chatting or playing games on their mobile or ipads. The day dragged on and at last it was time for final break. Larna sat outside in the sunshine with an ice cold can of orange and day-dreamed. Gradually, she began to relax. She hoped she and Aron would be allowed to leap into the future again. But would it be from the same place and the same time-frame with Tiblou and friends? Or would they land in the middle of a whole new heap of trouble somewhere else with other powerful warlocks and Boggrets and who knows what else hell-bent on killing her and her brother. In spite of the warmth on her face, she shuddered at the thought of the perils they might face as she made her way back into class for the final forty-five minutes before home-time.

Just as their form tutor, Miss Sismey, was entering the room, a rush of wind from an open window slammed the classroom door in the woman's face and shattered a pane of glass. Her cries of pain brought hurried footsteps and, holding a handkerchief to her bloody nose, she was led away. The room erupted in boisterous chatter, the class divided between those who felt sympathy for the strict teacher and those who felt it was a sad start to her holiday. Then the door opened and in walked Mr Waight, restoring order just by his sheer presence. He didn't look much older than some of his students but he possessed an enviable talent for commanding respect and holding the interest of everyone in attendance. He said that he would supervise them until the bell that everyone was longing for finally rang. Larna was looking at the weather forecast on her mobile and missed the knowing look between the teacher and quick intake of breath from Jonty who was sitting next to her.

CHAPTER TWO

RETURN TO SHERWOOD FOREST

After an eternity of waiting, the bell rang at last and pandemonium broke out in every classroom. In Larna's, chairs scraped back on the parquet floor and loud, happy chatter drowned out Mr Waight's voice. His shout of *'Quiet!'* was disregarded, so he gave an ear-piercing whistle. Immediately, everyone fell silent and stood still.

'Take all your possessions with you,' he ordered. 'Remember, next term somebody else's backside will be parked on those seats.'

'Warn 'em not to sit on Mia's chair, sir,' piped up some joker at the back, 'It smells.'

A great shout of laughter went up at this. Then a female voice added, 'Don't listen to him, sir. Pete's chair is the one to avoid. All he ever eats for lunch is baked beans and farts.' More laughter followed this and lots of high fives amongst the girls.

'Okay, okay.' Mr Waight chuckled. 'Go on, get out of here...' and had to shout again... *'Enjoy your holiday, most of you have earned it...and don't do...'*

With one voice the students finished his sentence, *'...anything you wouldn't do...'* Then they all rushed for the exit.

Halfway out of the door, Larna looked back. She wasn't the last to leave the room. Jonty was standing by the window with Mr Waight. They were deep in conversation, but stopped and turned when they realized Larna was still there. Both looked worried, but managed to force a smile.

'I'll be out in a minute, but if I don't catch up with you have a great holiday,' Jonty called.

'You too. I'll text you when I get back from my hols, as my gran has lots of plans for us and I may not have time to message.' she called back and then realized she'd left her phone on her desk. Smacking her forehead to show how stupid she was, she hurried back between the rows of empty desks to retrieve it. She was so intent on doing this that she failed to notice the room was getting darker. Thin strands of smoke had begun to appear from the four corners of the ceiling and were wafting down, attempting to coalesce above her head. In a world of her own, Larna snatched up her phone and stuffed it into her bag.

'See you later,' she called over her shoulder, and hurried outside into the sunshine to wait by the gates for Aron. Had she looked back, she would have noticed Jonty and the teacher watching her through the window – Mr Waight's face wearing the same expression of deep concern that it had when he'd walked past her house at midnight. The two of them were well aware of the smoke but could do nothing about it because it swirled round them, paralysing them with cold. They remained motionless, eyes staring, their breath coming out in puffy white clouds.

Unable to find Larna, the spectre curled up into itself and took shape. Then the ghastly spinous creature went hunting for her. Windows rattled and the classroom door banged shut again with even more force than before when Miss Sismey was injured. Searching the corridors in vain and realising its prey had escaped, the evil presence lost cohesion and returned from whence it came. This second attack proved that the warlock, Mordrog, was not behind the spectre attacks, as Larna had imagined.

Eventually Aron burst out of the building, his backpack slung over one shoulder, and raced across the playground to join his sister at the gates. Within fifteen minutes they'd walked the short distance home. Dropping their schoolbags in the hall like and happily changing out of their boring school uniform, they grabbed their customary snacks and marched back upstairs to play games on Aron's computer until mum came home.

That night Larna was restless and kept bashing her pillows to get more comfortable. Even so, sleep eluded her. The sky was unusually black and starless and her thoughts began to wander. They oscillated between excitement and fear. One minute she was thinking of Tiblou, their young wizard friend, and Cai the handsome shape-shifting Undine from the other mysterious world below Sherwood Forest. Next moment she was remembering all the terrifying ordeals they'd faced during the first trip to the future and niggling doubts about the forthcoming holiday crept into her brain, squirming like worms on a hook. Unable to stand it any longer she crept downstairs, heated a mug of milk in the microwave and took it back to bed. A few minutes later the house and its occupants were all peacefully asleep, blissfully unaware that in less than thirty-six hours' time, the teenagers would be caught up once again in the deadly dangers that lurked in the seemingly peaceful world of Sherwood Forest.

* * *

The following morning, Larna conveniently forgot the bad vibes she'd suffered during the night. Everyone was up bright and early, washed, dressed, breakfasted and impatient to be on the road. For a change Larna wore her hair tied back in a scrunchy, the shorter sides curling down over her ears. This went well with her jeans and white wolf t-shirt, to remind her of Tiblou. Just as casual, Aron wore jeans and Hollister top. Both were excited at the prospect of a second visit to their grandmother's amazing house in the forest.

Mum stood by the front door twirling her car keys. 'Get a move on,' she called upstairs, 'or we'll hit the rush hour traffic and be late arriving at Blithe Cottage.'

Larna double-checked her travel bag, determined not to forget anything especially her Smartphone and printed geocache clues. Suddenly her heart skipped a beat - they weren't where they were supposed to be! She rolled her eyes as she remembered removing them from the main backpack and zipping them into one of the secret pockets inside for safe keeping.

With a final impatient call from their mum ringing in their ears, Larna and Aron grabbed their things and raced downstairs, dropped the lock on the front door, banged it shut and sprinted to the car. Hurling their bags into the boot they jumped in, did up their seat-belts and set off, their spirits soaring. The traffic wasn't too bad and within forty-five minutes Elizabeth turned off Blithe Road and onto a private track lined with magnificent lime trees that led through Clumber Park and ultimately to her mother's cottage in the forest itself.

'Hope we don't encounter another freak storm here like we did last year,' commented Mum. These triggered memories for them all of Clement, a mysterious figure who had appeared from nowhere looking as ancient as the forest in which he lived. Larna and Aron now knew he was the guardian of the portal that allowed them to time-travel into the future, but not a word of this was mentioned to their mother. Sitting side by side on the back seat, Larna and Aron found their thoughts returning to their first visit, remembering some of the happy times that had stayed with them since last Easter. Uppermost in Larna's mind was Cai, her shape-shifter friend from the future Sherwood. *Maybe* ... just maybe... they would meet again. Unfortunately, that would mean she'd have to go deep underground to the lower world where he lived and risk being captured by the Boggrets, a race of evil creatures whose cruelty was beyond belief.

She gave an involuntary shudder. Aron on the other hand was more predictable. *Food!* He was remembering Roger's Café, an amazing eating-house belonging to Tiblou's uncle where every dish on the menu was strange and exotic. He remembered chasing some green rolling pasta round his plate. When the pasta ran out of steam, he had a split second to wrap it round his fork and quickly shovel it into his mouth before it began rolling again. Then the flavour hit his taste buds in wave after wave of delight. Aron wished they had food like that in this century. With a sigh, his hand rested on his stomach and smiled smugly.

Unaware her children were far away, lost in their thoughts, Elizabeth gave a grateful sigh of her own. No fallen trees or broken branches were strewn in their path to block their way this time. And no sudden apparition of a strange elderly gentleman to redirect them on their way. Last year had been weird. This year everything was normal.

* * *

Twenty minutes later they turned right onto Neve's drive. The car wheels crunched on new gravel and, as they approached the cottage, Elizabeth pipped the horn to alert her mother of their arrival. The front door opened wide, Neve sauntered out and stood on the top step, hands on hips. She was wearing a yellow short-sleeve blouse tucked into a flowing blue floral skirt with a shiny red belt. To complete the outfit, she wore a large brimmed straw hat and a broad smile. The car skidded to a halt sending a shower of gravel into the air. The teenagers held their breath as a large stone flew upwards and would have hit Neve smack in the face had she not raised her right hand as if in a wave and deflected it by magic. It happened so fast without her daughter noticing a thing. But the grandchildren saw and Neve gave them a knowing wink. They both grinned and winked back.

Neve marched down the steps towards them.

'You have no idea how long I've looked forward to this holiday,' she said, embracing the teenagers fondly. She bent to whisper in Aron's ear, 'I heard your stomach growl twenty minutes ago, so I knew you weren't too far away!' Then she said to them both out loud, 'I'm sure you could eat a horse - unless you've suddenly become vegetarian. So scoot! You know where the kitchen is.'

They were about to dash into the cottage, but came to an abrupt halt when Mum called, 'Oy, you two! Have you forgotten something?'

She raised the boot of the car and thumbed the inside. 'Duty first! With long-suffering groans Larna and Aron hurried back, grabbed their bags and then hoofed it towards the savoury smells.

'I haven't forgotten you, Lizzy,' added Neve. 'Hot apple pie with a dollop of Cornish ice cream suit you?'

'Oh mum,' she groaned, patting her stomach, 'You are *so wicked.'*

Neve laughed, 'Elizabeth, love, you have no idea.'

CHAPTER THREE

THE GUILTY SECRET

It was good to be back at the cottage, but this time something was different. Both Larna and Aron felt it but neither could fathom out what it was. Instead of worrying, however, they shrugged it off, went to their respective bedrooms and unpacked their bags.

Suddenly, Larna's eyes glazed over. She placed her fingers to her temples and pressed hard. Her eyelids fluttered and closed as she stood facing the open window, her back ram-rod straight. She could hear a faint knocking. Rhythmical. A succession of strong then weak tapping sounds. Tinny, like something imprisoned and trying to get out. A cold draft of air blasted through the window sending the curtains billowing inward, hitting Larna in the face. Her eyes shot open and her vision cleared. The look of surprise quickly turned to horror. She remembered. *THE WAND!* Of course – that's what was wrong! She'd spent the last fifteen months pushing the problem to the back of her mind and, at home, she'd almost succeeded. But it hadn't gone away.

The wand had belonging to the deceased warlock, Mordrog. It had been taken by the power-hungry Boggret, Edsel, and had secretly attached itself to Larna, who had unwittingly brought it back to the present at the end of their previous trip. Terrified of its awesome power, she had told Aron and they had buried it in an old biscuit tin in the forest without telling anybody. Not even Neve. This was *their* secret and theirs alone. But just thinking about it made her knees buckle and she flung out her hands to break her fall as she sank to the floor, instantly riddled with guilt and foreboding. Was she and her brother being naïve? Could a wand so full of evil magic remain hidden for long? Clearly it wanted to be found and was doing its best to make its presence known.

Staggering upright and sitting shakily on the bed, she tried to think logically about the situation. Was it time to confess all to Neve? Larna knew that burying the evil thing and, *worse*, being secretive about it was bound to cause a great deal of trouble. Not just here and now, but also for their friends in the future Sherwood. She reasoned

11

that even though it *hadn't* been her fault that the wand had travelled back in time with her - this didn't solve the problem. Confession is good for the soul, they say, but what if they were banned from vitsiting Sherwood for the rest of their lives? What would happen then? Try as she might, she couldn't seem to find a way out of the dilemma. Say nothing. That seemed the best solution.

Vaguely she heard Neve calling that their mum was about to leave and to hurry downstairs if they wanted to say goodbye. Larna was in a turmoil, half wanting her mother to stay but half-knowing it was out of the question. She had to wish her mother well and let her drive away believing all was as it should be and that a good time would be had by all. Aron leaped down the stairs two at a time and raced out to the car. Larna had trouble moving her legs that felt as if they were in a sticky morass. When she eventually emerged into the sunlight her mother was shocked.

'Are you alright, love? You look very pale.'

Larna knew she didn't look her usual self, but also knew the reason why. Crossing her fingers behind her back she opened her mouth prepared to tell a lie. But Neve quickly cut in.

'She's fine, Lizzy,' she said with a smile. (No one else would dare call Elizabeth, Lizzy.) 'Tiredness, I expect. A bit of rest and recuperation and lots of fresh Sherwood air. She'll be as right as rain in no time at all.'

'I can stay tonight if she's not well...'

Neve realized Larna's white complexion was becoming an issue and jumped in again.

'No, Lizzy love,' she insisted. 'That's not necessary. You go! It's too late to change your plans now.'

Elizabeth knew she was fighting a losing battle with her mother, so gave in gracefully. After hugging Larna and Aron and kissing Neve on the cheek, she climbed into her car and pulled away. The three of them stood and watched as she drove down the drive, right arm out of the window waving. Neve stood silently with an arm round each of her grandchildren's shoulders until the car turned and was gone from sight. Simultaneously, there were three loud exhalations.

'That was a close call,' Aron said.

'No parting lecture about staying safe this time either,' added Neve. 'Either her memory's going or we're getting better at not being caught.' Without another word Neve ushered the teenagers back into the warm, comfortable kitchen just as the grandfather clock in the hall chimed twelve mellow beats. It seemed to signify all was well...

just for now, anyway.

* * *

They sat round the kitchen table, each with a drink of their choice.

'Now then, you two, it's time we had a chat,' said Neve in her usual no-nonsense manner. Aron opened his mouth to speak, but she held up her hand. 'I want the truth, now. No holding back. Remember, I know when you are trying to be...shall we say... economical with the truth. Who's first?'

Larna's blood ran cold. She thought her grandmother knew about the wand. But the old lady only wanted to know how they had coped with the trauma of their previous visit to the future.

Aron started the ball rolling. He told her about his bad dreams, reliving his nightmare experience of being pulled into the vortex of a well when he was under Mordrog's spell. At the time he thought he would die and every dream relived that horrifying feeling. Talking about it made his mouth dry up, so he took a quick sip of his juice. 'I'm not too bad now,' he added. 'In fact, I haven't had that nightmare for quite a while. The other one that still comes back is when I saw Larna disappearing into the ground and I couldn't dig her out. I honestly thought she was a gonner and I thought I would be too if I returned without her.' Another sip. 'But it worked out okay, didn't it? She's still here for me to annoy.'

Neve turned her head and looked directly into Larna's eyes. She waited, not needing to utter a single word.

Taking a deep breath, Larna began. 'I feel as though part of me has changed since we returned from our first leap into the future,' she explained. 'Such a lot happened to us there - some bad, some very bad, but a lot of good came out of it too! We met some amazing people, didn't we? Okay, as Aron's said, at times I thought I was a 'gonner' too. Falling through the earth into the underworld of Sherwood was terrifying, but if I hadn't done that I wouldn't have met Cai.' For a few seconds she appeared wistful and her lips curled up in a slight smile. 'He helped me out of the caves and up through the Major Oak to the surface again. At great personal risk, I might add. He saved me from an army of Boggrets who were trying to kill me...and him. One of his own people died protecting me.' She stopped for a second. 'Another thing. You know Annie, Tiblou's mother? She would still be wondering what happened to her husband Zebediah and his sister June if I hadn't been to the underworld. '

Neve said, 'Don't you realize that everything happens for a reason?' Then she asked, 'Have either of you had any form of communication with Tiblou since your return?'

They shook their heads. 'OK, then. Let's continue. How have you been during the past fifteen months, Larna?'

'Fine thanks, Gran,' she replied. Then she stopped, wondering how much to tell. 'Oh, heck! You'll read my mind anyway. I expect you'll think I'm imagining it, but often I get the feeling I'm being watched. When I turn round, there's nobody there. That's when a tingling sensation runs down my back. Weird!'

'Go on,' Neve prompted.

'I've noticed that my teacher, Mr Waight, and my friend Jonty seem to be keeping tabs on me. Just recently I've seen them in a huddle whispering about me and I'm never alone for very long, in or out of school, before one or the other turns up. I know it's crazy, but I can't shake off the feeling they're shadowing me in some way. What do you think?'

Neve leaned across the table and patted Larna's hand. 'You always did have a vivid imagination, Larna love.' But she wasn't smiling.

Getting bored, Aron decided it was time for a change of tack and cut in, 'What I'd like to know is...' he paused for effect... 'where did *your* powers come from?'

Her burst of laughter broke the tension. 'In my case, I was born with it. My mother, Clara, your great-grandmother - also had the gift. Most of my female line was either born with special powers or they were gifted to them when the previous witch died. The same applies to wizards and warlocks.'

Aron made a cross with his fingers and hissed at the mention of warlocks. Neve disregarded Aron's levity and carried on, 'In fact, I can trace my family, via the female line, back hundreds of years.'

'So what about us?' Larna asked excitedly. 'Have either of us inherited any powers? How can we find out?'

'Do you wish to find out?' replied Neve, her face grave. 'With superpowers comes great responsibility and they can be deadly in the hands of a novice.'

After that, the three sat in silence, finishing their drinks. Larna's complexion was back to normal and she was just beginning to relax when she heard tapping again. Strong and then lighter - TAP, TAP, TAP. Tap, tap, tap. Her eyes rounded in shock. She gripped the edge of the table until her knuckles turned white. Her face drained of its colour again. But the others did not appear to hear it, so Larna decided to say nothing. Having just been told she had a vivid imagination, she didn't want to be accused of making things up again. But she was sure it was the wand. After a little while, the tapping stopped and she gave an inward sigh of relief. The colour returned to her cheeks.

'I think I'd like to go out for a breath of fresh air if that's okay, Gran,' she said. 'Coming, Aron?'

'Yeah, okay.'

'Good idea,' agreed Neve, leaning forwards to pour herself another cup of tea. 'We've done enough talking for now. Go and stretch your legs.'

In the past, Larna and Aron had needed permission to go through the garden gate into the forest, but they felt they didn't need it any more. They walked in silence for several hundred yards, then *CRACK!* It sounded as though a gun had fired. Larna's heart lurched. What now? Not more trouble! She turned sharply, but they were alone. *SNAP!* There it was again. They both stopped, turned and frowned.

'Who's there?' Larna called anxiously.

'I heard you two were due about now, don't ya know,' replied a familiar voice.

Looking all around, Larna and Aron spied a big black crow with a plumage of red on his head perched on a branch above their heads.

'*Clem!* We should have known!' Aron groaned. 'You frightened the life out of us, don't ya know.'

Clem flew down. 'Now then, Master Aron,' he scolded, changing into the old man of the forest, with his mass of carroty red hair, 'no need to be taking the mickey.'

'How's your sister, Clementine?' Larna wanted to know. 'Is she still guarding the other side of the time-portal?'

Before he had time to reply, there came the sound of footsteps and Neve appeared.

'Just making sure that all is well.' she said, glancing at Larna and Aron.

Clem bowed. 'All's well, Neve.' He bowed again.

Neve laughed, 'Clement, my old friend; stop bowing man, you'll give yourself a nasty crick in the back. Actually, for a change, I thought I'd walk home with my grandkids.' She stopped, her right hand behind her ear, listening. She turned to Larna and Aron, a quizzical look on her face. Then she put a finger to her lips, shushing them. 'Can you hear a tapping noise?'

This time Larna thought all was lost, but Clem came to her rescue without realizing it.

'It must be a woodpecker,' he said. 'There's plenty about this year.'

Feeling very relieved, Larna walked quickly on until they reached the cottage. She glanced backwards in time to witness Clem morphing back into his crow persona and flying away into the forest. Aron seemed to have forgotten about the wand. So she decided not to tell him what she believed was really doing the tapping. And she hoped against hope that the wand would realize it wasn't going to be recovered by any of them and go quiet again. As long as Mordrog's evil wand remained buried in the ground, nothing bad could possibly happen and their worrying secret would remain safe.

CHAPTER FOUR

AN EVIL VISITATION

Neve resurrected an old gong from the glory hole under the stairs. She only had to hit it once. The sound reverberated up the stairs and into the bedrooms, startling Larna from her reverie. She hurried down in an attempt to be first at the table. Near the bottom she looked back in time to see Aron sprint to the top of the stairs, slide down the banister and race past her into the dining room before she could grab him. A triumphant grin on his face.

'Dammit!' she muttered, bashing the newel post with the flat of her hand in frustration.

The three of them sat down to dinner helping themselves to succulent roast lamb, pear halves cooked in mint sauce, new potatoes, mixed vegetables and corn-on-the-cob with melting butter running down the sides. After a suitable wait for the first course to go down, Neve produced hot lemon meringue pie. When she served a dollop of ice cream on the top of each portion, it immediately began to melt and form moats round the sides.

Aron noted it was static. 'Wish it was Uncle Roger's speedy sauce,' he murmured, visualizing himself in the future, chasing it round the dish with his spoon.

The rest of the evening passed by pleasantly until the ancient grandfather clock in the hall began to whirr and chimed ten mellow beats.

'That's it, you two, away with the Scrabble,' commanded Neve. 'Last one in bed cooks the breakfast in the morning–*and* loads the dishwasher afterwards.'

Within seconds the plastic letters had been tossed into a green cotton bag and shoved into a drawer along with the board. Not to be beaten this time, Larna pipped her brother to the bottom of the stairs, but was yanked back. Amid noisy laughter they jockeyed for position, crawling up each step on their hands and knees and pulling each other back. They carried on like this until they reached the top.

'All right, all right,' Neve called from the hall below. 'You've had your bit of fun. Now it's time for some shut-eye. Go on, the pair of you, and for this little carry-on you're both on breakfast duties.'

Still laughing, out of breath, they prepared to argue the toss, but Neve silenced them just by waving her finger. Then she launched herself into the air. With a bit of a thud her slippered feet touched down on the landing ahead of them. Chuckling, she turned towards her bedroom which she called her Inner Sanctum.

'Night, night, love you.' she called. 'See you in the morning, nice and early.' Her door closed silently and a sign in bright red began to scroll across the middle panel:

But NOT before seven.

Then it bled away.

Larna and Aron separated and entered their own rooms. Larna flung herself on top of the covers, hands clasped behind her head, and began daydreaming about Cai with his smooth face and gentle voice. It was so quiet, except for the distant hoot of a night owl and the natural creaks of the cottage settling on its foundations, Larna felt herself slipping away. It was warm, comfortable, so pleasantly relaxing... but, moments later, she sat bolt upright, her heart pounding. She felt woozy, disorientated. Her vision began to blur. She sensed rather than saw something on the wall at the bottom of the bed trying to take shape, moving towards her. Her eyelids felt heavy and she fought to keep them open, managing only a little vision. No, not one but two figures were coming at her from out of a white mist on the wall. Then she thought she heard Aron calling, 'G'night,' followed by a loud bang as he back-kicked his bedroom door shut. She blinked and shook her head hard, coming back to reality.

There was no sign of anything untoward having happened in the room. But her head ached like crazy and she felt a bit sick. Slowly, she slid off the bed and tiptoed along the corridor past her grandmother's room.

Descending the stairs, she took extra care to step over the wonky treads so as not to make a noise and crept into the darkened kitchen. Her bare feet cool on the tiled floor. After pouring some filtered water into a glass, Larna made her way back, pausing momentarily outside Neve's room because she heard a rustling noise and a faint cry which was cut off abruptly. She put her ear to the door and listened. Silence. Just her wild imagination playing tricks again. She padded on.

Feeling dog tired, Larna dropped her clothes in an untidy heap on the floor, put on her pyjamas and crept under the covers. She'd play it safe and tell Neve about her weird vision in the morning. Her head had barely hit the pillows before she felt strange again. There was something going on here tonight. Two figures were trying to materialize from a whirling mist. Identical twins? All she could distinguish were two grinning faces, the bodies seeming unable to take shape from the freezing ectoplasm which wafted from their skulls. Even the faces kept changing. One looked angelic, the other evil. Then they'd swap. Larna tried hard to concentrate but couldn't tell which was which. Girl or boy? Boy or girl?

From the bottom of the bed, the covers began to stiffen and crack as ice formed and crept upwards towards Larna. Feeling cold as it moved towards her she began to shiver. The room grew lighter as crystals of frost formed and spread. Larna realized that the duvet was now freezing, becoming rigid. She tried to scream but was shivering so much it just sounded like a feeble croak. All the time the faces smiled at her, one angelic, one evil, and then they swapped again. Mesmerised by their eyes, Larna realized she would soon be incapable of movement. Even breathing. Tears froze on her cheeks mid-flow as she waited for the inevitable to happen. She'd be entombed within her own body. She'd die a horrible death. She couldn't let Neve and Aron find a frozen corpse in the morning, she had to try and fight back by shifting her limbs. But the only part of her body that would move were her teeth. They rattled violently making a peculiar sound like distant clacking.

Suddenly all the crystals started to explode, like lights going out, and the substance which emanated from the twins vanished. The two faces looked at each other and glared. From one of the down-turned mouths drifted the words, 'One down, Refina.' And one twin disappeared.

'Still two to go though, Rufus.' said the other, also fading into the darkness.

Next moment, Aron burst into the room and pulled the duvet off Larna's prone figure.

'Wake up. *WAKE UP!*' he shouted. 'It's gone eight. We've overslept. I've searched everywhere, inside and out, and I can't find Yaya!'

The instant Larna opened her eyes, realization dawned that she was not frozen solid, nor was the room covered with ice crystals. So why did she feel so cold? She began to rub her arms for warmth. Sitting up, a shudder rippled through her entire body.

'The sun's blazing outside,' cried Aron. 'How come your room's freezing cold?'

'I think I had a visitation last night. And before you ask, I've no idea who or what or where they came from. Now go and have another look for Yaya while I get dressed.'

* * *

Aron ran back down the corridor and banged on Neve's door, calling her name over and over. By the urgency of his tone, Larna instinctively knew her brother wasn't joking. She dressed hurriedly in the crumpled clothes she'd left on the floor the night before. Given the nightmare she'd just experienced, she too felt seriously alarmed.

A loud cry of distress from Aron spurred her into action. Racing down the corridor in her bare feet she joined her brother at Neve's bedside. Her teeth began to chatter and her exhaled breath froze like fine vaporized mist. So did Aron's. This room was now freezing cold. Ceiling and walls glistened with thousands of frozen crystals caught momentarily in the sunlight that shone through the partially open window. Then a cloud hid the golden rays, plunging the room into gloomy darkness.

Larna closed her eyes, remembering that this horrific scene was identical to the one she had experienced herself. Was it just a nightmare or had it been real after all? There was no way of telling. Their grandmother lay under a homemade patchwork quilt, her arms on top. She looked peaceful as if asleep. Larna lifted one of Neve's wrists and felt for a pulse. She tapped the arm trying to get some form of response but it was hard like a lump of ice. Shocked, she dropped it back onto the covers. It bounced, not even denting it. That was when she sniffed the air and picked up a whiff of cloves. It was a strange smell, full of menace. The hair on the back of her neck stood on end and a sudden rush of fear almost brought her to her knees. Aron stood mute, looking at his sister, his eyes wide and staring.

'*Larna!*' he screamed.

A shadow had appeared behind her. Turning slowly, she was just in time to see the body of one of the grinning faces begin to form and slowly solidify from the ectoplasm swirling around it.

'Your turn, 'Fina.' said the first laughing head.

The rest of the substance stabilized and a second grinning head appeared, a young female, almost identical to the first. The body solidified in the same way. She stood behind Aron, one hand on his shoulder. He looked like a living statue, unable to move or speak, his skin turning grey. Only his terrified eyes showed a spark of life.

'*This* time it's going to work,' the female said triumphantly. Then she nodded at Larna. 'That one *really* put up a fight!'

20

'Ru, you are an *idiot!* The element of surprise came very close to failing because you insisted on a dummy run with … *her!* So don't you go…'

Out of the wall stepped an older, more mature female. First came the flowing black hair, then slanting green eyes set in a scarred face. Then followed a skinny body inside an ankle-length purple garment. It was obvious the three were of the same family by the way the twins deferred to the woman. Behind the woman came a small ugly creature that rattled when it moved.

'Rufus, Refina, behave yourselves!' she commanded. Then the woman stepped behind the girl twin who was holding Aron hostage and removed the offending hand from his shoulder. Immediately Aron dropped to the floor, cowering with fear, then scrabbled as far away from the trio as possible.

'*Who are you?*' Larna demanded. 'What do you *want?*'

The woman smiled. A cruel smile which only made the scar running down her left eyelid and cheek more inflamed. Her long hair flew about her head like Medusa's serpents, crackling with energy charged by her anger.

'*I* am Edina. These two ruffians,' she said with pride, 'are Refina and Rufus. And this is Selka.'

'What have you monsters done to our grandmother?' cried Aron, still on his hands and knees in the corner of the bedroom. Edina raised her right hand which held a smooth black wand. It seemed to pulse in time to her heartbeat. Her cat's eyes became slits, blazing with intense hatred, and then just as quickly returned to normal. Her hand dropped to her side after sliding the wand into the folds of her gown. Pulling herself up to her full height, she spat, 'They have only done to her what she once did to me.' Her lips thinned in a malicious grin, crooked and poisonous. 'A favour returned, you might say.' Then she threw back her head and laughed, a painfully high-pitched shriek that caused Larna and Aron to cringe and clap their hands over their ears. The twins thought this was hilarious and joined in while Selka bounced up and down on the spot with glee. The room rocked with a cacophony of unearthly sounds. Seconds later, Edina lost interest. And patience.

'Oh, for crying out loud,' she growled, inclining her head towards the bed. 'She's perfectly alright.' She scattered a fine spray of red mist into the air which, on impact with the walls, began to explode the ice crystals. 'For the moment anyway.'

The girl, Refina, stepped forward. The only way to tell the

twins apart was by their hair. The girl's hair was long and black with purple streaks, her brother's, short and spiky; though he had a strip of purple hair hanging down each side of his face. Larna peered anxiously at the woman's right arm, hoping she wouldn't produce her black wand again. Of the three, she looked the most powerful and the most unstable.

'I see you've taken an interest in Mama's wand, Larna,' Refina stated, waving her arm in a circular motion. Larna's eyes followed the girl's magic staff as she twirled it round and round like a cheerleader's baton. Suddenly, she remembered the wand she'd accidentally brought back through the portal the previous year. Her stomach lurched and her chin dropped to her chest to hide her flaming red face.

t whooped Refina, punching the air, 'She remembers!'

'Like ... a certain wand she stole and brought back tot this century?' Selka added with a gloating sneer.

'We don't know what you're talking about,' said Aron, shooting his sister a warning look. Fearing these foul creatures might be able to read their minds, he willed her not to think about what they'd done. They'd soon get busted if they pictured the tree under which they'd hidden Neve's biscuit tin and its deadly content. At home in Doncaster, Aron had managed to forget about the wand as he went about his daily life. Now, back in Sherwood, with these evil creatures reminding him about it so gleefully, the memory came flooding back. Like his sister he hoped their terrible secret would never be exposed. But now it seemed that it might. And he was scared stiff.

CHAPTER FIVE

THE CRYSTAL OF SOULS

A soft moan reminded Larna and Aron that, even though the room temperature was returning to normal, Neve was still incapacitated and they remained in grave danger. Aron was the first to regain a modicum of confidence and blurted out, 'If that wand belonged to who I think it did, then I say good riddance. He was a monster.'

For a few, silent seconds the air in the room seemed to tremble with emotion. Edina and the twins drew themselves up, casting dark shadows over their enemies, and Selka's slimy skin glowed with hatred. Four pairs of eyes bored furiously into Aron and Larna.

'Mordrog was my **Brother!'** screamed Edina, 'He was not a monster. He was clever and powerful and our protector. Even that pathetic old wizard, Balgaire, was aware of my brother's strength and feared him.'

'Oh, get it over with, Mama,' urged Refina. 'Just kill them all. Do to them what Uncle Mordrog did to that old duffer, Balgaire.'

A slight movement from Neve didn't go unnoticed. She was beginning to rouse from the icy spell into which she'd been cast, struggling but failing to open her eyes. The black wand appeared in Edina's hand again. She began to wave it in slow circles over Neve in the bed, clicking her fingers to make sure Aron and Larna were paying attention.

'All you have to do is tell me where my brother's wand is and we will leave as we came,' she snarled menacingly. 'If you don't... well...what price your grandmother's life, eh?' She tapped the end of the bed. The vivid scar on her face pulsed a mesmeric beat. Fearful for Neve's life, Aron moved to the side of her bed, opposite his sister, and nodded his assent with a deep sigh. Larna had to agree. They had no choice but to admit defeat. She opened her mouth to describe the burial place, but...nothing came out.

Next moment, a ball of black feathers tumbled through the open window. It began to grow and change shape into Clement, guardian of the gateway to the future. He stood directly in front of

Edina, preventing her from carrying out her threat. He held out his hands, fingers curled tightly around something.

'Edina, take your brats and your hideous servant and leave,' he said in a cold voice.

With an angry yell the twins prepared to launch themselves at Clem's ancient body and Selka rattled his tail like a snake about to strike. Unfazed, the old man opened his hands to reveal a large azure crystal. Natural light from the window reflected off the many facets and shone round the room. When Clement raised it directly in front of their faces, Edina put a warning hand on Rufus and Refina's shoulders, stopping them from taking further action, and called Selka to heel like a dog. The crystal moved, looking alive. Edina peered closely and jumped back in horror when she saw what was inside the clear blue glass. Visibly shocked, she pulled the twins closer to her side and yanked the chain round Selka's neck when they attempted to glimpse what was in Clément's hand.

'Just leave!' ordered Clem. 'Heed my warning. If you don't, the crystal will claim your tormented souls like those in here.

In their ignorance the twins couldn't understand why their mother had given in to the old man's threats so easily. Neither could Selka. They were all angry, puffed up and determined to fight. But Edina's hands were still resting on their shoulders and she gave the twins a violent shake before glaring furiously down at Selka. The three of them looked back at her, seething with indignation. Then she nodded, her eyes reddening as she shot a terrifying look at Larna and Aron. An unspoken threat that she would be back. They had unfinished business!

'You may have won this time, old man,' she said to Clement, 'but you won't best me again. Those kids owe me and I intend to collect what is rightfully mine.' With that Edina stamped her foot and clapped her hands three times in rapid succession. A purple mist billowed out of the wall behind them. Turning on her heel, shoved Rufus and Refina, still bitterly complaining, into it and dragged Selka after them. They all disappeared. The choking vapour and Edina's body smell of cloves followed suit.

Feeling numb with shock, Larna felt rooted to the spot. Her face screwed up in bewilderment, as in *Help! What just happened here?'* Surprisingly, Aron appeared the calmer of the two, which made Larna feel weak and helpless and, therefore, extremely uncomfortable. Moving to the bed, Clem held Neve's right hand in his left and began whispering what sounded like gibberish. Time seemed to sloowww...riiight...dowwwn and so did Clem's voice which deepened and slurred. Neve opened her eyes and very slowly eased herself up into a sitting position. As she shook her head to clear it, time and motion speeded up again until it had returned to normal. Turning to her grandchildren, she acknowledged them with a gentle smile.

'Although I couldn't see or move,' she explained, 'I wasn't totally incapacitated. While my brain was still functioning, I was able to use telepathy to summon help.' Neve turned to Clem and drew a deep breath. 'You came alone which was foolhardy to say the least, but we *are* very grateful Clement. You jeopardized your own safety to save us.' She paused. 'How on earth did you *manage* to send Edina and her brood packing?'

A chuckle escaped Clem's lips. He opened his right hand and proffered the crystal. Aron and Larna leaned forward to nosy.

'What's wrong with it? It's lost its sparkle.' Aron wanted to know.

'Nothing is wrong,' their friend answered. 'It's just that there are no wicked souls to be collected in this room now.' He grabbed Aron by the hand and rolled the stone onto his palm. 'Here, as you're so interested, you take charge of it for a while.'

Aron snatched his hand away, dropping the stone in horror. **'No!'** he squealed. 'Not on your life. There are...*things* ...wriggling inside, trying to get out.'

The old man bent down, picked up the crystal and groaned. Putting a hand on his lower back, he rubbed the ache. 'No, there aren't,' he said patiently. 'It's empty now. What you saw were evil souls, removed from evil people. When Edina and the twins left this room, so did they. Into...' he waved his hands in the air '...oblivion. Once empty, it shuts itself down. It's perfectly safe to touch, don't ya know.'

Neve shoved back the covers and swung her legs out of bed. 'How did you manage to get hold of the Crystal of Souls? I haven't seen it in years,' she said.

'Tiblou heard your call for help and, as I'm already in this century, he sent me.' He raised his arm, the crystal shone. 'And he sent this.'

'Just as well you knew how to use it,' commented Neve.

Clem shrugged and pulled a face. 'I didn't,' he confessed. 'It was already primed for action.' The Crystal began to tremble and gradually fade away as it returned to Tiblou.

'*Awesome!*' Aron exclaimed, his hands still hidden in his trouser pockets.

Smiling, Clem said, 'Yes, it is. And I'm relieved I'm not responsible for its safe keeping any longer. Well, mission accomplished. I expect that you three have a lot to discuss, so I'll bid you farewell.' He looked knowingly at the teenagers.

Clem was just about to return to crow form when, on the spur of the moment, Aron rushed forward and embraced him. Clem was embarrassed, but also extremely touched. He bowed deeply, rubbed his back again, returned to bird form and, unlike his entrance, departed in a more dignified manner.

Larna hadn't noticed Neve's attempt to stand up until, out of the corner of her eye, she saw her wobble and grab the edge of the headboard for support.

'I guess it will take a little longer to coordinate,' she sighed and fell heavily onto the bed. She was obviously in more than a little pain from thawing out and the feeling returning to her extremities. She lay back on the pillows and sighed. 'You know; Clem was correct about one thing. We do need to have an in depth chat!'

Panic coursed through Larna as she remembered Mordrog's wand. Attempting to change the subject, she asked, 'Can I get you a cup of tea?'

'You can get me some water and a couple of pain killers. I have a thumping headache.'

Aron followed his sister downstairs into the kitchen. As they searched the cupboards for the medication he asked, 'Do you think she suspects anything?' Furtively, he glanced behind towards the stairs and whispered, 'You know, about Edsel's wand?'

'It's looking that way. I wish we'd fessed up straight away, as soon as we realized the damn wand had followed me back through the portal. What a cock-up, Aron!' A tear slid down her cheek. '*Now* there's going to be trouble.'

CHAPTER SIX

THE DANGEROUS TRUTH

Neve stood at the window, deep in thought. She looked stronger and her colour was returning. The tablets had taken away her headache, but she still felt weak and tired. She sat on the bed again.

'Give me an hour and then we'll have that chat, OK?' she said, kneading her temples. 'Whatever you do, don't leave the house. Is that understood?'

'Yes, Yaya,' Larna and Aron answered in unison. Shamefaced, they retreated downstairs to the kitchen.

The next hour seemed interminably long. They did their best to sit quietly, but Aron's left foot nervously tapped the floor irritating his sister and Larna's intermittent pacing and sighing got on Aron's nerves. They squared up for an argument. But the creak of a loose stair tread told them they were about to have company and so they immediately forgot their irritation with each other. Neve slowly entered the room looking pale and wan, though her eyes seemed more focussed.

'How are you feeling?' Aron asked.

'A little fuzzy-headed, but apart from that I'm fine. I've changed my mind about that cup of tea, if you don't mind?'

Larna had never made tea so fast before. The kettle appeared to be alive, coming to boiling point within seconds. It didn't occur to her to question it, accepting it as the norm in this house. Placing the tea in front of Neve, she took her place at the table and waited in silence, dreading what was coming next.

Looking straight at Larna, Neve began, 'I think you know why we need to talk, don't you?' Eyes cast down, Aron and Larna nodded dumbly. Neither said a word. Where to begin? 'All right then, I'll start the ball rolling. Something untoward happened to one of you last year as you returned to your own time, didn't it?' Silence. The hapless pair looked miserable. 'Since your last visit I've sensed an atmosphere. A shift in the order of things. Whatever it is you've done, you must tell me.' She waited for one of them to explain. 'You mistakenly think I can read your minds all the time. Well, I can't here. So please help me out.'

Aron had never seen their grandmother so agitated. He was frightened and knew his sister must be as well. But still they said nothing. 'Clem knows now, doesn't he?' continued Neve. 'And I know Edina was in my bedroom, as were the twins. My hearing was fuzzy, so I was unable to hear every word! They weren't there for the fun of it. They wanted something. *What **was** it?*' she was fast losing patience with them.

Larna looked at Aron's frightened face. It was time to come clean.

'I've been wanting to tell you this for ages, but was too scared. I didn't do it on purpose, I swear. I'm so sorry, Yaya...' She broke down in sobs.

'*Out* with it, lady. What exactly have you done? Come on, ***tell*** me.' She took a deep breath. 'Whatever it is. I shall remain calm.'

Finally, Larna blurted out, 'On our last return from...you know where...I brought something back that should have remained in the future.'

Neve sat forward, elbows resting on the table, head on fists. '*Well. And...?*'

'I brought back Mordrog's wand!' with shoulders raised, head down prepared for a tongue-lashing as Larna's face drained of its colour.

Neve inhaled sharply. She slumped back in the chair and for a few seconds was devoid of speech. Then she whispered, 'Have you any idea of the danger you've placed us in?'

'*I didn't do it on purpose,*' Larna wailed. 'I didn't even know I had it until we went to bed that night. We buried it in the forest in one of your biscuit tins.' The silence was painful.

'It all makes sense now...' murmured Neve. 'That explains why Edina was here with her brood. She's after the wand that belonged to her brother. And it also explains why you couldn't remember where you hid it. Tiblou must have found out about this and blocked that memory.' She shook her head in despair. 'I must get a message through to him immediately.' Decision made, she stood up and produced a wand from her skirt pocket. 'I need you to remain in this room. Is that understood?'

Aron and Larna nodded, miserable, and afraid to disobey. They'd never felt their grandmother's wrath before. She swept out of the kitchen, like a teacher leaving an unruly class, and the two of them sat in silence wondering what was going to happen next. They did not have to wait long. Suddenly, what sounded like an ear-piercing scream rent the air.

'Was that Yaya?' Aron gasped, gripped by fear.

'If it is, it sounds as if she's in deep trouble again,' gulped Larna. Her brow furrowed. 'I don't care what she told us, I'm going to find out what's going on - whether you come with me or not.'

'But what if it's another trick? She was very emphatic about us staying put.'

Next moment...**BANG!** The house shook violently. Everything that wasn't a fixture fell to the floor, including Aron and Larna.

'Oh my God! Oh my God! We're gonna die!' wailed Aron.

'Stop panicking!' snapped Larna. Her tone was sharp: she was fighting hysteria herself. 'Nothing's going to happen to us. Just stay by my side, OK?' Looking at the mess on the kitchen floor. They listened, all was silent again. Larna said, 'We'll clear this up later. I think the coast is clear now. Come on, we must go and find what's happened.'

They crept out into the hall. It was freezing cold. They both knew what that meant - Edina had returned. Larna looked around. Everything had fallen down, including the grandfather clock, which had stopped ticking. An eerie silence filled them with foreboding. Aron's eyes were wide with fear and he had to keep reminding himself they were doing this for their grandmother. They tiptoed around, picking their way between the debris calling her name for the second time today. But there was no answer. They searched every nook and cranny of Blithe Cottage over and over again, but they knew in their hearts she wasn't there anymore; and neither was her wand. Edina must have taken her. But *why?*

* * *

Larna and Aron sat together in the icy kitchen, not knowing what to do. Should they phone their mother and ask her to come back? That would mean telling her everything, which would be a disaster and, what could she do anyway? They could try to find Clem, but that would mean venturing far into the forest and neither of them felt like doing that. They were in enough trouble already.

They were in the depths of despair, shivering uncontrollably from a mixture of cold and fear, when suddenly the room became lighter and warmer. They looked at each other in astonishment, sensing that something was about to happen, and jumped to their

29

feet in excitement as the air began to buzz and shake.

'Yaya's coming back!' whooped Aron.

'I'm afraid not,' said a familiar voice. 'It's me.'

With relief and delight, Larna and Aron saw the friendly face of Tiblou materialising in front of them. It was followed by the rest of his body, wearing a smart mystic green coat robe with a mandarin collar that made him look older and more powerful than when they had last seen him. But his face was the same with its large green almond-shaped eyes and the dark blonde mop of shoulder-length hair.

'Oh, Tibs!' cried Larna, rushing over to hug their friend with relief and joy. Understanding their feelings, Tiblou didn't need to read their minds to know what they were asking.

'I don't know where your grandmother is,' he answered. 'But I know she must be in trouble. She reached me a short time ago and started to explain about Edina's visitation when contact was suddenly terminated. I already know about Mordrog's wand...'

'It wasn't my fault!' cut in Larna, desperate for Tibs not to be angry too. 'The wand attached itself to me and travelled back in my pocket.'

'It's okay, Larna,' soothed Tiblou. 'Really it is. Evil has a way of surviving, so you're not to blame. But we must do something about what's happened. I believe Edina has taken your grandmother prisoner and won't release her until you free the wand.'

'Here we go again, Edsel kidnapped her last time, Edina this time!' said Aron.

'Correct,' agreed Tiblou. 'The witch was frustrated that a memory spell stopped you from telling her the whereabouts of Mordrog's wand, so she came back and took your grandmother. She will kill her unless we reveal the secret.'

'Oh my God.' gasped Larna, her face turning white.

'We must act as soon as possible.' Said Tiblou 'Edina will have taken your grandmother back to her domain, so we need to leave here immediately and try and find her.

'Visit the future again, you mean?' said Aron.

'That's exactly what I mean,' replied Tiblou. 'Get your stuff and be ready to go in five minutes. I can return there directly, but you two must travel through the portal as you did before. Clem will guide you. I'll be waiting for you, in my time. So hurry now.' Then his face softened and he smiled at the worried looking teenagers. 'Relax,' he said. 'You're not on your own anymore.'

CHAPTER SEVEN

A BUNDLE OF GREY FEATHERS

It was with lighter hearts that Larna and Aron set out into the forest now. They knew what they were doing, where they were going and that friends were waiting to help them. Larna used the GPS facility on her new phone and followed the geocaching directions she'd brought with her to locate the spot in the tiny clearing between the ancient trees where they'd been before. As promised, Clem was waiting for them. He was in crow form, looking down from a high branch, but he morphed into his human form as he flew down and landed on the ground beside them. But he was not as cheerful as when he'd visited Blithe Cottage.

'This is a bad business, don't ya know,' he said, handing Larna the red jewelled key that he had guarded for centuries. Then he nodded at her to begin. She knew what to do, chanting **ELLA VITA, ELLA VITA, ELLA VITA** in a loud clear voice. Immediately, the ground began to shake and they heard the familiar rumbling sound as a large block of stone rose out of the ground in front of them. Then a red glow appeared in the rock and Larna knew to insert the key into the hole it had burned. The heavy stone door opened inwards and they stepped forward, turning to wave a brief goodbye to Clem before disappearing through the portal and into the future.

Clem's twin sister Clementine was waiting for them. She led them away from the portal towards a wooden bench where Tibs was sitting with Violet, the Gothic fairy, who was fluttering round his head like a giant butterfly. The visitors had forgotten how striking she was. Only eight inches tall, she had the heart of a lion and the courage to match. Sometimes her eyes were bright green; on other occasions they became coal black. The tip of her nose pointed up and she had masses of long, wavy purple hair which framed her delicate features.

'Welcome!' she said. 'It's good to see you again.'

But there wasn't time to say any more. The sky clouded over in a matter of seconds and big fat raindrops began to splash all around.

'We've chosen the wrong moment to arrive,' cried Larna. 'I forgot it always rains at the same time of day here.'

'We're gonna get soaked,' wailed Aron, pulling his top up over his head.

'Not if we run for it,' laughed Tiblou. 'Come on, you two. This way!'

Leaving Violet sheltering under an overhanging rock, her delicate wings no match for the mighty raindrops, they put their heads down and raced off through the downpour.

'You ok, sis?' Aron shouted.

'Course I am,' Larna retorted. 'I'm fitter than you are. I don't spend all my time sitting around playing computer games.'

Charging round a corner, Larna stopped dead in her tracks. Aron barrelled into the back of his sister, giving her an almighty shove. Both of them nearly fell over. But they didn't quarrel because they were faced with an awesome sight.

'I guess you weren't expecting this,' said, Tiblou, grinning broadly.

'*Wow!*' whispered Aron.

About a quarter of a mile away stood the most amazing building Larna and Aron had ever seen. A small castle-like dwelling. It had two pointed towers with silver roof tiles which guarded each side of the entrance. The main door was partly hidden by a massive weeping willow tree with a thick trunk and many branches. The windows in each tower were slim and from a distance seemed to stretch from the ground to the top. Both towers were pale green but, the main building appeared to be a rich blue, matching the flags fluttering on the highest point of each tower.

'Who built this?' wondered Larna.

'I did, but with a lot of help from the Grand High Council.' answered Tibs. 'From Balgaire's sketches. While rummaging through his belongings, I found a rolled-up drawing with my name on it. I felt I had to uphold his final wishes.'

They were soaked now and couldn't stand and stare any longer. They rushed towards the front door and the shelter of the big willow tree. With the rain sliding off the downward-pointing leaves and dripping steadily onto the ground, it really did appear to be weeping. But it was dry underneath and the front door was sheltered, as if by a giant umbrella.

'Clem loves this old tree,' commented Tiblou, patting his robe in search of his wand.

'I thought he was stuck in our time,' queried Aron.

'Clem lives in every time,' explained Tibs, 'past, present and future, although, officially he's not supposed to time travel. He first came into existence way back in the period that you call The Middle Ages, around the year 1200. Have you ever heard of the Earl of Loxley?'

'You're not trotting out that old fairy tale about Robin and his Merry Men, are you?' Aron scoffed. Larna put a restraining hand over her brother's mouth, scowling at him to shut up. She fondly remembered her time in the underground caverns with her shape-shifter friend, Cai, (pronounced Ky), during their first visit to the future and escaping from the murdering Boggrets through the middle of the Major Oak. When they'd parted, Cai had told a tearful Larna, 'If you believe in Robin of the Hood, believe in dreams-and of me.' She did dream of Cai! Often!

She pulled her thoughts back to the present as Tibs continued, 'Clem and his sister Clementine are from that era, but because they fell afoul of a sorceress whose powers helped the cruel Lord of the manor, they were condemned to a timeless existence. As the centuries came and went, Clem stayed in yours, his sister went forward into ours. It was The Grand High Council who gave them their ability to change at will into crows on condition that they guard the keys to the monoliths in both Sherwood's.'

Tibs noticed Aron beginning to fidget. He was cold and wet and wanted to go inside. So he produced a wand that was green with a gold twist, aimed the tip at the heavy oak door and flicked his wrist. It opened silently and closed smoothly behind them as they hurried through. As he did so, his impressive robe was replaced by his usual shirt and trousers.

'Useful spell that,' he said with a grin. 'Saves me having to get changed.'

Then a hot wind blew through the hall. Tibs told his friends to hold their arms out and turn round in it. Their clothes were dry in a matter of minutes.

Feeling warm and comfortable again, they gazed at their new surroundings. Except for a large chromium-framed portrait of the deceased wizard, Balgaire, the walls were very high and bare. Larna, ever the sensitive one, shivered as the dead wizard's eyes seemed to follow them everywhere. Standing in the middle of the hall, she saw that each of the two towers had stone spiral staircases. The main wooden staircase led up to the next level from the middle of the hall. In the recesses there were four light oak doors which perfectly matched the stairs and banister.

Tiblou marched in front, manually opening one of the doors on the left. Aron and Larna followed him into a good-sized sitting room. There was a large stone fireplace on one side. Set back in the alcoves were two old-fashioned windows with leaded lights. The glass was stained and showed wild flowers so that, when the sun shone, a rainbow of colour filtered into the room. Placed in this light were some comfortable high-backed carved chairs. And there was a large portrait of Tiblou's family over the fireplace. Larna went over to look at it. There was one face she did not recognise.

'Isn't that your father?' she asked. 'You have his eyes.'

Before Tibs had the chance to answer, the door burst open and his mother Annie bustled in, looking her usual cheery self. She embraced both visitors. Then she too looked up at the portrait and her face clouded over into a wistful smile.

'One day...' she sighed, 'one day we'll be able to mount a search for their father in the underground caves – provided the Boggrets don't catch us before we find him. Or what's left of him.'

They were interrupted by scratching on an adjacent door. Larna was on the verge of ducking behind Aron when Tiblou's face broke into a smile.

'There's someone I would like you to meet,' he chuckled, crossing to the door. 'My friend is quite harmless, so there's no need to be frightened.' He'd only half-opened the door when he was nearly flattened by a bundle of grey feathers. Fighting the creature off, he spluttered, 'I should mention he can get really excited?' The big bird settled at Tiblou's feet and a pair of beady eyes settled on Larna and Aron. They scuttled backwards.

'What kind of creature is *that?*' gasped Aron.

'It's a Swooper!' Tiblou explained. 'In the wild they're very dangerous, but this poor chap was a runt and unable to defend himself when he was attacked by his siblings. He tried to fly away but went smack into a tree. I found him, took him home and mended his broken wing. His beak was knocked out of joint, and one of his legs needed a splint too. He couldn't fend for himself nor could he be set free. In the end he adopted me.' He bent and patted the bird's head. 'His name's Ozzy.'

The bird began to make high pitched purring sounds each time his orange paddle beak opened. It waddled over to Aron and rubbed its neck against the leg of his trousers. Nervous at the best of times around animals, Aron stepped back a pace. But Larna, the nature-lover, bent down and began stroking Ozzy's head making him purr even louder like a contented cat.

Annie decided that her usefulness lay in the kitchen making everyone a drink. As she left, Ozzy waddled out, chasing her. He was obviously after food because she could be heard laughing and scolding the Swooper like a naughty child. Then Chet entered the room. He was Tiblou's brother, two years older and three inches taller, who was another friend of the visitors. Shaking his shoulder length brown hair out of his eyes, he held out his arms and embraced them both warmly in turn. For a few seconds there was a lull in the conversation. Chet glanced from one to the other, sensing that something was amiss.

Aron looked beseechingly at his sister. So she stepped forward, put her hands on her hips, 'Right!' she said. 'Now that we've said hello to everyone, can we *please* formulate a plan to search for my grandmother?'

CHAPTER EIGHT

MIRROR, MIRROR ON THE WALL

Outside the rain had stopped and the sun was shining again, making the lawns and flowerbeds surrounding Tiblou's castle steam like a sauna. Violet flew in through the now open window and perched on the back of a chair, eager to join the meeting and hear what was to be decided. The others sat around, sipping the drinks that Annie had brought them, waiting for Tiblou to begin the discussion. But before he could open his mouth to speak, something caught his eyes. He whipped round and stared at the grate. The others all gazed in the same direction. The dead embers in the fire grate had moved slightly. A lump of cinder fell onto the stone hearth and began to grow. Tiblou pointed at it, Chet gasped in surprise, a small scream escaped from Annie's throat, Larna and Aron paled noticeably and Violet just watched, fascinated, as the lump of burnt coal grew into a squat, with scaly bluish green skin. It continued to take shape, its ugly face and a rattling tail coming into focus.

Aron and Larna realized it was Selka. They went to warn the others, but there was no need. Tiblou had drawn out his wand and was pointing it at the being like a defensive weapon. Chet pulled everyone behind his brother and Violet hovered in the air above them, waiting for something to happen. At first, the creature only had eyes for Tiblou. Larna guessed that at some point in time the two had a history. Not good. Stepping away from the hearth, Selka scratched himself and an acrid smell of fish permeated the room. Larna slapped a hand over her mouth and pinched her nose to prevent herself from being sick. Aron, whose stomach was made of sterner stuff, just watched as the scene played out in front of them.

The cultured voice, so totally at odds with the creature's physical appearance, resonated round the room like a speech from the stage. 'I have been charged to pass on a message from my mistress, Edina,' he intoned, pausing for effect as he saw the fear register on the faces of everyone in the room. 'If you do not comply with her wishes, you will never see the white witch, Neve, again.' Another pause. 'Alive or dead.'

The room went still and silent. Nobody moved. Realising his

theatrics were not having the desired effect, he produced a scruffy sheet of paper and waved it in the air. Tibs raised his wand and held out his hand. The creature opened his fingers, letting the paper go, and it fluttered across the room onto the wizard's extended palm. Mission accomplished, Selka retreated onto the stone hearth with a final gloating look at everyone and began to shrivel back down to a coal again. When the reverse transformation was complete, Tiblou used an ornate pair of tongs to pick up the cinder, but he dropped it and a few bits flew off. He tried again and successfully placed it among the other burnt coals and ash in the grate.

Aron was the first to find his voice. 'We've seen that disgusting creature before. Who and what is he exactly?'

'Selka,' Violet said.

'A Kappa,' explained Tiblou. 'A very ancient type of malevolent semi-human creature associated with water. Some are harmless; others are not. Selka is definitely not. He's very dangerous – cruel, clever and slippery. Literally *t* slippery.'

'What's in the letter?, Chet asked.

Tiblou read the contents to himself, shook his head slowly, tut-tutted and said, 'Just as I thought - though I expected a bit more originality from the woman.'

Before the last syllable was out of the wizard's mouth, one of the broken pieces of cinder became translucent and started to swell until it reached the size of a beach ball. It rose slowly into the air, bobbing rhythmically up and down at Tiblou's eye-level. Everyone watched, their heads moving in time with the sphere, waiting for what would happen next. Suddenly the object became transparent and the scarred face of Edina appeared within the globe.

'I didn't think you would take Selka seriously so I came in person...so to speak.' She gave a harsh laugh which made her cough. 'You've read my note. My terms are simple and quite clear so that even you can understand.' She paused, waiting for a reaction...any reaction, from any of them. When there was none, her face flushed with anger, her eyes became slits and she pursed her lips. 'My brother's wand in exchange for Neve, Sherwood's white witch,' she spat out. 'And, if you need proof that she is still alive...' Edina vanished and a dishevelled Neve, trussed up and gagged, faded in. She looked old and tired with dark smudges under her eyes. Her hair was a tangled mess and some strands had caught in the tape over her mouth.

Edina's wand came into view and raised Neve's chin. She looked half asleep, or drugged. 'There! See! She's perfectly alright.

For the time being anyway. But she won't be for long. So jump to it.' Having issued her ultimatum, Edina and Neve disappeared. The cinder sphere popped, spraying foul smelling sulphur on anything within range. Then it vanished.

'Has she gone?' Aron gasped.

'Yes,' replied Chet. He turned to Tiblou. 'What was in the letter?'

'Here, see for yourselves,' said Tibs, handing it round to the others

THE WAND IN EXCHANGE FOR NEVE. BRING IT TO THE BRIDGE AT MY CASTLE IN THE VALLEY OF ICE BY THE NEXT BLUE FULL MOON. OR SHE DIES.

'Where's the Valley of Ice?' asked Aron.

'It's a desolate place a long way from here,' replied Chet.

'And how long until the next blue full moon?' put in Aron.

'A few days, give or take,' answered Tibs, grimly. 'But it's only people with magic, like your grandmother and myself who can sense when a blue moon is due to rise. Also, Edina's castle, in the valley of ice, is within a magic dimension, and the days and nights are very much shorter. The moon is blue for one hour only.'

The worried expressions on everyone's face was too much for Larna.

'This is all *my* fault,' she burst out, hitting her chest with a closed fist.

'Don't be so melodramatic, Larna,' scolded Annie. 'You know very well that you were the innocent victim the wand attached itself to you to escape being destroyed forever. It's no good beating yourself up about it, the deed is done. All that matters is that Neve is found as soon as possible.' Out of breath and words, she sat heavily on the chair opposite Larna.

'She's right,' Tiblou soothed. 'I told you that before.'

Ozzy waddled over and put its beak on Larna's knees, making a soft throaty sound. Without thinking, Larna began to stroke the bird's head and neck, accepting comfort from the soft downy feathers of the tame Swooper.

'Apart from the wand,' said Chet, 'her hatred of us all seems totally irrational.'

'On the contrary,' Tiblou replied, 'it's easily explained. We were responsible for defeating Mordrog. Edina has sworn to avenge her brother's death and to do that she has to get his wand back. We are the people standing in her way. So we are the enemy – her hated enemy.'

Everyone nodded in agreement. Then, despite her best efforts to stifle it, Larna gave a yawn. It had been a long day and she was getting tired. Aron looked dead on his feet.

'It's getting late,' said Annie. 'There's nothing more we can do tonight, so I prescribe some sleep for us all. Things will look better in the morning.'

No, they won't have sighed Larna. We still haven't thought of a way to rescue Neve without giving in to Edina's demands.

* * *

No one slept well or wanted any breakfast. This worried Annie, so she insisted everyone should go to her brother's café for something to eat.

'No one can operate on an empty stomach,' she explained. They all knew better than to argue. When Annie made up her mind about something, there was no shifting her. So, instructing Ozzy to guard the house and asking Violet to stay with him to deal with any possible trouble, she marched out through the woods with everyone in single-file behind her.

Roger and a girl about Aron's age came out to greet them. She was petite with shoulder length mousy hair and blue almond-shaped eyes. She smiled shyly at them and especially at Aron. Roger introduced her as Elva, a local girl who was learning the catering trade. She was no relation of the café owner, but she called him Uncle Roger and he treated her like one of the family. Shyly, she helped to show everyone to their seats before hurrying back into the kitchen.

Aron and Larna were surprised to see that the place had changed drastically since their last visit. It was now Americanized with red and white booths and red vinyl seating. Large ornate mirrors, in keeping with the period, adorned two walls and instead of posters there were pictures of Roger's regular customers smiling down from the walls. This was to celebrate the happy outcome of Larna and Aron's last visit when they had given blood which had reversed rogue DNA and restored the local population to their human selves. Hung on the back wall was a family portrait of Annie, Zeb and very young Chet and Tiblou. There was also a portrait of Roger and his sister June. Like his sister Annie, he now sported a more rotund figure, but looked comfortable with it. He still had his old animal tail. It was a little shorter now and a little worse for wear because he didn't hide it any more.

'I think they like the changes you've made here, Rog,' said Annie.

'I like it' said Aron as he and Larna shuffled round the table and into one of the booths, feeling quite at home. Picking up the large menu, Larna found her appetite had returned and she ran her finger down until she came to something she fancied. 'Blueberry Oatmeal for me, please,' she said. Aron decided he'd also like to try the same thing with a glass of sour apple.

'Make that five for Blueberry Oatmeal Roger,' Annie said.

Moments later, the food arrived in flying bowls that whizzed round the room like miniature flying saucers landing gently in front of each of the guests.

'Wow! That's *so cool!*' Larna smiled, then remembered her grandmother's plight and felt sad.

Aron didn't comment. He was too busy eating. The mood round the table became a bit more positive whilst they were getting warm food into their stomachs. But their appetites would have disappeared again had they known what was really going on.

Edina was watching them secretly through one of the mirrors. Consumed by her evil thoughts, an unpleasant smile froze on her face.

'Is something troubling you mistress?' asked Selka.

'Shut up, Selka,' snapped the witch. 'I'm listening.'

'Would you like me to listen too? Would that be of assistance to you?'

'NO!' shouted Edina, pushing the creature away so he fell over on his back and struggled to get upright again like a gigantic overturned turtle. 'What I'd like you to do is go away and leave me alone. I'm trying to hear what these fools are saying. I want to know their plans so I can stay one step ahead of them, understand?'

'I understand, mistress,' puffed Selka, finally managing to struggle upright and backed away into a dark corner to avoid any more abuse.

Meanwhile Refina and Rufus were amusing themselves taunting an almost unconscious, bound-and-gagged Neve behind the second mirror. They forced her head up so she could see Larna, Aron and their friends in the cafe who were totally oblivious of being watched. Even though she was in obvious pain and distress, Neve's eyes tried to focus on Tiblou, desperately trying to get his attention.

But Larna and Aron were sitting opposite Tibs and Chet, blocking her weak signal. Willing the young wizard to stop talking for a minute and Larna to move out of the way, she attempted to send another telepathic message to tell them where she was.

The signal pulsed through Larna. She kept rubbing the back of her neck and looking round the room. She shivered. 'Can anybody feel a draught?' Nobody answered. They were too busy talking and finishing their Oatmeal. 'Someone must have walked over my grave, then,' she murmured, shivering and rubbing her neck again. She began to feel dizzy and disorientated. All colour drained from her face and she grabbed the edge of the table for support. Her lungs wouldn't expand enough to take in a deep breath and she thought she was going to pass out.

'I need to get some air,' she gasped, starting to slide sideways.

Chet pushed Tiblou out of the way just in time to catch Larna before she hit the floor.

CHAPTER NINE

A DEADLY RIDE

Larna became aware that she was moving, swaying gently from side to side, being lulled into a comatose state. All she wanted to do was sleep, cocooned in a dream world, but at the same time, she was being pulled upwards towards a bright light and noise and visions of her grandmother in distress calling her name. She felt trapped and afraid.

'Larna...' the faraway voice called. 'Larna...open your eyes...'

She tried. With difficulty she managed to open one eye, closed it again...and then jumped as she opened them both and sat bolt upright.

'What happened? Where am I?' she whispered, the colour gradually returning to her face. Taking stock of her surroundings, she realized she was back with her friends. They were all standing around her, looking very anxious. She was sitting on a seat outside the café.

'Are you okay?' asked Aron, anxiously.

'I th-think so...' stuttered Larna, struggling to her feet.

'What happened, dear?' asked Annie. 'You look very pale.'

'I had a vision of Yaya calling to me, she's in desperate trouble.'

'Then she must be somewhere near!' exclaimed Tiblou, excitedly. 'She was trying to communicate with us and tell us where she was.'

Breathless with excitement, everyone watched as Tibs stood motionless, pressing his fingers to his temples he sent out his own telepathic message to Neve. But after a while he looked at the others and shook his head. 'No answer,' he said, wearily. 'If your grandmother was nearby with Edina and her foul brood, they're all long gone now.'

Everyone felt their spirits drop and they began to trudge back to the castle. As they reached a small crossroads, a clip-clopping noise was heard in the distance and a strange vehicle came into view. It was a replica of an old-fashioned four-wheel horse-drawn carriage. But minus the horses. They were just a sound-effect. The interior was royal blue velour with arm rests piped in gold that pulled down between the passengers for their comfort. The exterior was shiny burgundy.

'Roger must have sent this to take us home,' said Chet.

'That's funny,' commented Annie. 'He didn't say anything to me about providing exotic transport for his customers.'

'Maybe he's trying it out on us,' suggested Aron, eager to climb aboard for a ride in the gleaming burgundy coach. But, remembering his manners, he stood back politely to let everyone else in first. He noticed that the vehicle seemed to expand as each person climbed inside and sat down, as if it could change shape at will. Even so, there was no room for him on the seats and so he clambered up the narrow ladder at the back and sat on the roof seat like a coachman of old. As the coach pulled away, he looked back at the café from his high vantage point and caught a glimpse of Elva sweeping up outside the café. She looked up and smiled at him. Aron was smitten instantly and knew his sister would taunt him unmercifully about it later, after their life had returned to normal. Whenever that might be.

The carriage rolled on down the narrow path between the trees and then came to an abrupt halt, jerking everyone forward and back. Aron was thrown off the roof and was lucky to escape with no broken bones. The thick patch of ferns on which he landed saved him from harm. But Larna had seen him fall and leapt out of the coach to see if he was all right.

'I'm fine!' he insisted, scrambling to his feet and brushing down his sleeves.

Brother and sister were enjoying a laugh when they heard cries coming from behind them. Spinning round they saw that the others were trapped inside the coach. The arm rests that moved up and down had now criss-crossed and were keeping everyone in their seats. At the same time, the coach itself had started to shrink. Soon everyone inside would be crushed to death.

Larna rushed back to the coach, leapt in and tried to free Annie's arm rests. They wouldn't budge, even with the old lady pushing them. Neither would Tiblou's or Chet's. And every second the space inside grew smaller as the sides of the coach inched further inwards.

'Out of the way!' yelled Aron, yanking his sister back by her arm and scrambling into the coach with a thick branch of wood he'd picked up from the forest.

'Do Tiblou first,' called Annie. 'He's the important one.'

So Aron wedged the thin end of the branch under one of Tibs' arm rests and heaved with all his might. CRACK! The rest gave way and the wizard was able to scramble out of the tiny interior.

'Free Chet next,' ordered Annie. 'Doesn't matter about me.'

'It does, Ma...'

'Don't argue!' she shouted. 'We're wasting priceless seconds.'

Praying that the branch would not snap itself, Aron pushed it under Chet's arm rest and heaved again. Tibs and Larna cheered as they heard another **CRACK** and Chet wriggled his big frame out of the almost imploded coach. Aron was still working on Annie when he felt the roof of the coach pressing on his head.

'Keep going,' she urged him. 'There's still time.'

CRACK! With one final superhuman effort, Aron managed to free her and willing hands pulled them both from the closing coach. There wasn't a second to spare. Annie and Aron lay sprawled on the grass, panting for breath, as the coach squashed down to a tiny black ball and exploded with a deafening **BANG!**

'What the hell just happened?' whispered Chet in the eerie silence that followed.

'Somebody must want us dead,' replied his brother. 'And I'd put my money on Edina.'

* * *

Later, back at Tiblou's modest castle, everyone sat around nursing mugs of sweet tea to get over the shock. Violet did the honours because Annie was the worst affected. The busy fairy swooped around carrying the drinks and taking them away to refill. Before long, everyone felt marginally better.

'We must have a Council of War,' announced Tibs. 'With all these diversions, we're forgetting Neve is still in desperate trouble and we need to focus on thinking of a way to rescue her...'

Before he could get any further, the dead coals in the fireplace shifted again and a familiar form began to take shape. Stinking of dead fish, the apparition marched to the middle of the room as if about to give a command performance.

'What do you want now, Selka?' growled Chet.

The messenger, looking pained.

'Get on with it, Selka,' snapped Tiblou. 'We're busy here.'

'So I see,' the Kappa replied, looking round at the empty mugs. 'Anyway, to business.' He held out a note to Tibs, the movement of his arm sending new waves of fishy stench wafting round the room making both Larna and Aron gag. 'My mistress wanted me to deliver this to you personally, Tiblou Gorry.'

Tibs didn't offer to take the letter. He stood motionless, his gaze fixed on the smiling creature. 'I don't want to touch it. You read it.'

Selka's tail rattled twice in annoyance. Unable to fulfil his task, he was in danger of getting into trouble – painful trouble. 'Edina wishes you to know that she had nothing to do with the strange events of earlier today,' he announced loudly. 'And she wants to remind you of *t*.' He stepped forward and thrust the note into Tiblou's hand, folding the young wizard's fingers over it before hastily moving backwards, closer to his escape route. Tiblou pulled back in disgust as the creature touched his fingers.

'What does it say?' whispered Annie.

'Nothing we don't know already, mum,' said Tibs, screwing up the note and throwing it into the fireplace. 'Edina reminds us that problems like the one we encountered this morning must not deflect us from our true purpose which is to recover Mordrog's wand and deliver it into her hands within the stated time-frame. She has now retired to her domain in the Valley of Ice where she awaits our arrival within the next few days.'

'Er, so you'd better get a move on then.' put in Selka.'

Tiblou ignored him, his face contorting with unhappiness as he reported the final sentence.

'Otherwise, Edina says, the White Witch of Sherwood will die after the deadline, and we shall be frozen for all eternity – including you two.'

'Nice,' commented Aron.

'Yes, isn't it,' agreed Selka, a grin of delight spreading across his slimy face.

'Get out of here!' ordered Tiblou, pointing angrily to the fireplace.

'Very well,' agreed the Kappa. 'My mission is complete and I no longer have need of your delightful company. So I bid you all farewell!' With that he shuffled backwards towards the fireplace, his tail clicking from side to side. Moments later he was gone.

A long silence followed. Then Tibs stood up and smiled at everyone.

'Now, where were we?' he said.

CHAPTER TEN

WAND OF HOPE

Time is of the essence,' added Chet. 'The sooner we decide what to do, the sooner we can set about rescuing Neve.'

Everyone sat down and looked expectantly at Tibs. He appeared every inch the wizard he was destined to become. This morning he wore a robe of nature's green. He preferred to be casual, but he needed his official clothes and the power they conferred on him for the task ahead. But, for all his outward appearance, he felt powerless and was man enough to admit it. After a long pause he said, 'I really don't know what to do. I feel out of my depth.' and sat down.

There was a slight pause, then everyone started talking at once.

In shear frustration, Annie shouted, 'That's *enough!*' She looked at her older son. 'You go first, Chet. What do you think we should do?'

'I think we should fight Edina,' he replied, squaring up his shoulders as if he was about to take on the witch in single combat right there and then. 'We should travel to the Valley of Ice, ambush her and free Neve.'

'That's a great plan and typical of you, my dear brother,' sighed Tibs. 'But it won't work. Edina would know we were coming and ambush us first. She has amazing powers, remember. So we'd end up frozen for ever like she said. I don't fancy that, do you?'

Chet nodded his head in reluctant agreement and looked across at Annie. 'Who's next then, Ma?' he asked.

Before his mother could choose another speaker, Violet launched herself into the air and flew around in circles, glowing an entrancing purple colour as she gave her opinion.

'I think we should give in to Edina's demands...' she began, stopping with a look of anger as she was interrupted by a chorus of *'No!'* from everyone. 'Let me finish,' she continued frostily. 'As I was saying, I think we should give in to Edina's demands, get Neve safely back and then *defeat the evil witch afterwards.* We could combine our magic, mine and Tibs, and maybe look up some forgotten spells in the books Balgaire left behind. That should be enough. But you must remember, your wand may weaken the further we travel from the heart of the Major Oak'

Tiblou shook his head. 'The problem with your plan, Violet,' he said, 'is that you're forgetting one thing. Edina will have got her hands on Mordrog's wand by then. Her magic will be ten times stronger than ours - infinitely more powerful than anything we can command. There's no way we would be able to defeat her with that sort of weaponry on her side.'

'Hang on a minute,' frowned Aron, 'Won't their wands weaken as well?'

'No, because theirs are hued from the trees of Darkness. Which means they don't lose power the further away they are.'

'We could try...' protested Violet butting in, a flush of anger passing across her delicate features and making it almost shine like a mauve light.

'Don't get upset because your idea's been rejected, dear,' said Annie, soothingly.

'I'm not!' seethed the irate fairy. 'I may be small but I'm not a child, Annie. I miss Balgaire and I want every trace of his hated killer removed from the world for ever! Understand?' She floated down and perched on the back of a chair, fighting back the tears. The others said nothing. She was best left alone.

Annie, who seemed happy to continue in her role as chairperson of the meeting, looked across at Larna and Aron.

'What do you two think?' she asked. 'After all, it is your grandmother we're talking about and we know you both have a special bond with her.'

'That's the problem,' said Aron, getting to his feet as if he was giving a talk in class. 'We love and respect our gran and it's obvious you all do. So we just can't risk losing her. Although it goes completely against the grain, I think Violet may have a point we should give in to Edina's demand. I can't think of any other solution.'

Frowning, Chet asked 'Would Neve want that?'

'No, she wouldn't!' an indignant Larna exclaimed, jumping to her feet and taking the centre of the floor. 'That's defeatist talk. Anyway, I've had an idea. It just came to me. The way you're thinking is too black and white - either opposing Edina or giving in to her demands. But what about this...' She paused to look at everyone in turn before divulging her plan. 'Supposing we trick Edina into thinking she has Mordrog's wand? Then she'll release Neve and we can get away before she notices it's not the real thing.'

'Give her a fake wand, you mean?' said Tibs.

'Exactly!' cried Larna, her face alight with excitement. 'We find a dummy wand and decorate it to look exactly like Mordrog's. Then Tibs gives it some magic powers so it appears to be live and powerful. Edina will be so pleased to get her hands on it she won't notice it can't cast an evil spell until we're safely out of the way.'

'Brilliant!' exclaimed Tibs, slightly put out because he hadn't thought of it first.

'I second that,' agreed Annie.

'It's a fantastic idea. I just can't believe anyone as dozy as my sister could come up with it.'

This broke the tension, making everyone laugh. Tibs looked at Chet who gave a double thumbs-up sign at Violet who flapped her wings and clapped her hands at the same time, glowing with delight.

'So we're agreed, then,' summarized Tiblou. 'The plan is to deceive Edina by presenting her with a fake wand in exchange for Neve. Good thinking, Larna.'

'Please don't thank me,' replied the girl, collapsing onto her chair like a pricked balloon after the drama and excitement of the moment. 'I just hope it works. It will go some way to ridding me of the guilt I still feel, despite all you've said, about getting us into this terrible mess in the first place.

* * *

Problem solved, everyone felt hungry and thirsty now and so Annie busied herself in the huge kitchen, helped by Violet and hindered by Ozzy. Annie was busy buttering bread for an ever-increasing pile of sandwiches when there was an urgent knock on the heavy wooden door.

'Don't open it!' said Annie, suspiciously. 'Might be a trick.'

'Relax,' chuckled Violet, flying up to look out of the tall kitchen window. 'Anyone who's going to harm us isn't likely to knock first. It's your brother and he looks upset.'

Violet was right. Roger barely had time to greet his sister before making his way through the kitchen.

'I need to speak to Tiblou right away,' he said, hands on knees, out of breath. 'Where is he?'

'In the main room with the others,' Annie replied.

'Tiblou' he called, disappearing down the stone corridor between the two rooms.

Tibs knew something was up as soon as he saw how red faced and agitated his uncle was.

'What's wrong?' he asked, grabbing Roger's shoulders.

'I've made a discovery back at the café,' Roger blurted out. 'One of my mirrors has been changed. It's two-way now. About an hour ago I went into the storeroom, I could see into the café and hear everything my customers were saying. But if you're in the café, you can't see into the storeroom. It just looks like an ordinary mirror, the same as the other and, angled to where the kids were sitting.'

'Why does that matter?' asked Chet, scratching his head.

'Think I can answer that question,' put in Larna, holding one finger in the air. 'Remember I came over all funny earlier when we were having breakfast. I reckon there was somebody on the other side of the mirror. Probably Edina. I suspect she was spying on us, trying to find out what we intended to do.'

'That makes sense,' agreed Tiblou, pacing around rubbing his chin. 'And I reckon she had Neve with her as well. That's why you felt weird. Your grandmother must have been trying to send me a message, but you were in the way.'

'You mean Yaya was on the other side of the wall, just a couple of metres away from us, and we didn't know?' queried Aron.

'Looks like it.', said Tibs.

'That's so cruel!' sighed Larna, tears started to well up in her eyes.

 Roger looked up and started pacing round the room.

'You don't have any mirrors in here, do you?'

'No it's okay, Uncle,' said Tibs with a smile. 'No mirrors besides, my place is protected. Any intruder trying to spy on us would be instantly detected.'

'You know what this means though, don't you?' said Chet thoughtfully. 'If Edina is watching our every move, we can't just Aron and Larna need to go back to their own time and *t* to recover the wand they buried. Otherwise the cunning old bat will soon twig what we're up to.'

'You're right,' exclaimed Tibs, 'We should get going right away. I can transport myself back to the past, but Aron and Larna have to go through the portal. So are you two ready? The sooner we get started, the sooner we get finished, as mum always says.'

As if on cue, Annie marched in with two mountainous plates of sandwiches.

'Sorry, Mum, no time now,' said Tibs, hurrying towards the

49

door. 'Ready, Chet? You can escort Larna and Aron to Clementine and, I'll be waiting with Clem on the other side. Anything you two need to add?'

'Nope,' said Larna, shaking her head.

Giving everyone a bear hug, Roger said, 'Promise you'll all come back safely...otherwise...' choked up, he took his leave.

CHAPTER ELEVEN

ROOTS OF EVIL

Edina was pacing around her ice castle. It was in a desolate spot where nobody came, rocky and barren with frozen trees and icicles that hung all around like giant daggers. The clear protective dome which covered the whole of the future forest was frosted here, a permanent sheet of ice covering its inside making delicate patterns that contrasted sharply with the stark landscape inside it. The witch was impatient, pacing around muttering to herself, immune to the ice cold atmosphere.

At the other side of the castle, the twins were shouting at one another.

'*Be Quiet!*' Ordered their mother.

In temper, Rufus broke off a large icicle and viciously prodded Selka in the stomach.

Selka gave a loud belch and a sea of bright yellow half-digested fish heads spewed out over the twins.

'Stop doing that!' ordered their mother.

As the twins struggled outside to wipe themselves down and Selka hid to avoid being tormented further, Edina continued to pace backwards and forwards holding both hands to her temples. Then she stopped, giving a sigh of satisfaction, and stood perfectly still as she watched the scene that was playing in her head. It showed her enemies setting off on a journey. The two meddlesome Gorrys from the past were going somewhere with Tiblou.

'My guess is they're going to fetch the wand,' she muttered to herself. 'Now if we went too and watched them find it, I could snatch my property without having to exchange it for Neve. Then I could do away with the White Witch at my leisure and, unopposed, become the most powerful woman in the history of Sherwood. What a wicked thought!' She laughed and marched to the front of the castle. 'Rufus! Refina! Come here immediately. We're going back to Blithe Cottage.'

'Aw, must we?' complained the boy, wiping the last of the sick from his arm with a handful of melting snow.

'Yeah, it's boring there!' agreed his sister.

'It won't be this time, I assure you,' chuckled Edina.

The journey back to their grandmother's cottage proved himself there as he had done before while Larna and Aron went through the time portal with the help of Chet, Clementine and Clem. They found themselves standing together in the hall which remained untouched since they had left. It was late afternoon and the hot summer sun broken pictures.

'What a mess!' exclaimed Tiblou. 'What happened?'

'Edina,' said Aron. Just the name was enough to explain everything.

'Do you think we ought to tidy up a bit?' asked Larna. 'Yaya would be very unhappy to see the place in this state.'

'There's no time, Larna,' Tibs told her. 'We're on a mission, remember? She'll be a darn sight unhappier if we don't manage to free her in time.'

For the next hour and a half, they searched the cottage high and low for Neve's stack of spare wands. They didn't expect to find them easily, but it was proving impossible and they began to fear their plan would fail at the first hurdle. They were about to give up when Aron spotted a mouse scurrying down a hole in the floorboards in a corner of Neve's bedroom.

'Hang on a minute!' he called excitedly. 'Think I may have found something. 'The others hurried into the room and crouched down in the corner. Sure enough, there was a loose floorboard that Tibs lifted out gently to reveal a long thin chest with a hinged lid. Inside was a selection of powerless wands, some big, some small, some obviously new and some ancient-looking.

'This one looks the most like Mordrog's,' said Tiblou, selecting a large black one and tucking it carefully inside his cloak. Then he stood up and grinned. 'Mission accomplished. Time to go home.'

'This is home to us,' commented Aron.

'Don't be difficult,' chuckled the wizard. 'You know what I mean.' He marched towards the door, beckoning his companions to follow.

But Larna held up her hand. 'Wait,' she whispered. 'I just caught a whiff of cloves.'

Tiblou put a finger to his lips for quiet and for them to stay put. He silently made his way to the loft and crawled out onto the thatch roof in order to hear and scupper whatever Edina was planning.

Outside in the back garden, Rufus and Refina were examining a line of gigantic plants with flowers like open mouths that were springing up out of the ground all-round the cottage.

'What are these?' asked Rufus.

'Oh, who knows?' snapped Edina irritably. 'We haven't come here to discuss the flora of the ancient twenty-first century. Just leave them alone, will you?'

'But they're massive,' argued Refina, always one to defy her mother. 'And these flowers look like blood suckers. I want one, something new to torment, Neve, the old crone with when we get back home. That would be so cool.'

'*Leave it alone, child!*' hissed Edina, unable to shout like she wanted to because it would give the game away. 'Come over here and stand with me, will you. They'll be coming out any minute now.'

'Er, excuse me, mistress...'

Still angry and needing to stay silent, the witch ignored Selka.

'Mistress, I need to inform you...'

Again she took no notice of him.

'You *must* listen to me, Mistress...' he insisted, tugging her sleeve and received a powerful shove which sent him sprawling towards the giant flowers and one of them bent down towards him before he managed to scuttle away. Cowed into obedience, the twins and the Kappa waited in silence outside the cottage.

'Come on, *come on,*' urged Edina, tapping her foot impatiently on the ground. 'What's keeping you in there?'

Whilst on the roof Tiblou was having difficulty keeping his balance on the steep slope. The thatch was also very old and he worried he'd disappear down through it like Larna had previously disappeared into the underworld. But he managed to find a safe spot and, taking out his wand, he pointed it at the four figures below and chanted, **'*Expello tora!*'** On hearing this, Edina looked up and let out a scream of rage to find she had been outwitted.

'I did try to warn you, Mistress...' sighed Selka.

Next moment, the witch and her brood found themselves surrounded by a swirling vortex that lifted them up and carried them away into the distance. Their screams of terror and fury died away and the peaceful silence of a summer's afternoon returned to Blithe Cottage.

'Well done, Tibs,' said Larna as he came back down the stairs from the skylight in the attic.

'Thanks to you for sensing we'd been followed,' Tiblou came back.

'My sister always had a nose for trouble,' joked Aron.

'Well, at least we're safe now,' said Larna, opening the back door. 'Come on, you guys. Let's go home - as Tibs calls it.'

They stepped out in the garden and stopped in amazement.

'What the...?' gasped Aron.

The enormous plants were even bigger than before, forming an arch over the path that ran to the gate with their flowers leaning down and swaying back and forth menacingly.

'Have you seen these before, Larna?' asked Tiblou.

'No,' she replied. 'They're new to me.'

'Maybe they just grew here from seeds dropped by the birds or something,' suggested Aron. 'They're probably harmless.'

'They don't look harmless to me,' commented his sister. 'Perhaps Edina ...'

'No, she looked as puzzled as us. Well, we can't stand here all day talking about them,' Tiblou said. 'We need to get back.'

'You're right!' agreed Aron, marching boldly down the path ahead of the others. 'Let's get going and see what happens.'

Nothing happened, the plants stayed exactly where they were. He stopped at the gate and waved. 'Told you, they're harmless. Come on, you two.'

Larna followed her brother and nothing happened to her either. 'It's OK, Tibs,' she called. 'Aron's right. False alarm.'

But when Tiblou was half-way down the path, the plants attacked him with terrible ferocity. Hissing and squealing like angry animals, they leaned in from all directions, pulling at his clothes and wound themselves around him; the flowers began biting him with their snapping jaws.

The wizard's screams of shock and terror were stifled by another thick stem that wound itself round his neck and threatened to choke him to death in a matter of seconds.

'Wh-What do we do?' wailed Larna, her eyes wide with terror.

'This!' shouted Aron. He had noticed a wand had slipped out of Tiblou's gown as a result of the desperate struggle. Praying it was the wizard's and not the blank one they had just fetched from the cottage, he waved it in the air and repeated the words he'd heard Tibs pronounce just now. **'Expello tora Expello tora!'** he shouted, over and over again. The spell didn't work at first and the Gorrys thought they were about to witness the death of their friend, but suddenly the stem encircling the wizard's neck fell away and then the flowers lifted back, like troops being withdrawn from a battlefield. Next moment, the giant flowers withered away and disappeared into the earth leaving Neve's garden looking exactly like it had before.

Larna and Aron raced over to Tibs who lay on the ground clutching his throat and gasping for breath.

'Are you okay?' cried Larna.

'I think so,' croaked Tiblou. 'Just!'

Aron helped him to his feet. He stood on the path, looking very pale, and Aron rushed indoors to fetch him a drink of water.

'Thanks, Aron,' he whispered, his voice returning with his colour. 'I wouldn't be here if it wasn't for your quick-thinking.'

'What does that t mean?' asked Larna, curiously.

'Get lost...vanish!'

'What I want to know is – why did those killer plants only attack you? Why did they let Larna and I pass unharmed?'

'I don't know the answer to that,' said Tibs. 'Maybe we can work it out as we go back.'

'I have another question,' added Larna, lingering behind as the other two made their way to the gate. 'Who sent those deadly things to attack you, Tibs? If it wasn't Edina, then who was it? Then some other evil force must be at work here.'

CHAPTER TWELVE

THE HILLS OF AMBER LIGHT

Almost as soon as the trio returned, via their different methods, to Tiblou's future Sherwood, Tibs began to feel ill. It started with a sore throat and he thought it was just a cold. (Wizards are vulnerable to common viruses, just like everyone else!) But it was soon followed by bouts of terrible sickness and agonising pains in his arms and legs. With Chet's help Annie put him to bed and noticed huge red welts all over his body.

'Must be where those poisonous flowers bit me,' Tibs said.

'I'll fetch some ointment to soothe the sores,' said his mother.

But the ointment did no good. The wounds continued to fester.

'It feels as if I'm being eaten alive,' he croaked as the evening wore on, his face screwed up with pain and his forehead dripping with sweat. 'They must be carnivorous eating plants. Unless something's done soon, Mum, I've had it!'

Annie knew what to do. They needed help from Uncle Roger. Not only did her brother serve the locals with delicious food, he also acted as their apothecary, treating their ailments with a variety of ancient natural remedies he kept in a storeroom at the back of the café.

'I want one of you to find my brother and describe what's happened to Tiblou. He'll know what to do and send back the correct antidote.' Annie said to Chet, Larna and Aron.

'I'll go,' cried Aron, leaping to his feet.

'I'm a faster runner than you!' claimed his sister.

'Let me go,' begged Aron. 'I want to do it.'

And I know why thought Larna with a secret smile.

'Just choose and *go*, this is a matter of life and death.' cried Annie.

Seconds later Aron went racing off through the trees towards the distant café. The light was starting to fade, so he wanted to get there and back before dark. He arrived out of breath with a painful stitch in his side. He banged on the heavy front door, to no avail, so ran round to the back door and banged on that door too. As he hoped, Elva opened it. The pair of them looked at each other as if they'd both seen a ghost, then their faces blushed a deep crimson before Aron managed to blurt out, 'I n-need to see Roger. It's very urgent. Something bad's happened to Tiblou.'

Elva stood back without uttering a word, ushering him in then ran to find her employer.

Roger came bustling into the kitchen, wiping his hands on his stripy apron. 'What's wrong with Tibs?' he asked anxiously.

Aron told him about the deadly flowers and the terrible wounds they had inflicted on Tiblou.

'I've heard of these dreadful plants,' he murmured. 'Mordrog, ghastly creature that he was, used them as a weapon a long time ago. But the good news is there is an effective antidote...and I have the ingredients in the back. I just need to mix a number of herbal potions together and it will be ready, then you can give it to Tibs. Time is of the essence, though.'

He disappeared into the storeroom, leaving Aron and Elva alone together. Neither knew what to say to each other, so he just stood there looking at his feet and she went over to the sink to continue with the washing-up. But, at the same moment, they looked at each other and smiled.

Not long afterwards, Aron was racing back through the woods with instructions and the precious Medication gripped tightly in his right hand. Annie was waiting for him at the door, her face screwed up with worry.

'Where have you *been?*' she called.

'I'm back as quick as I can,' panted Aron, thrusting the phial into her hands.

Seizing the antidote, Annie hurried upstairs as fast as her matronly form would allow to give it to Tibs.

The hours that followed were endless. Despite the long day they'd just had, with the terrors of the collapsing coach in the morning and the terrible dangers at Blithe Cottage in the afternoon, Larna and Aron could not sleep. Like Chet and Violet, who paced and flew in opposite directions round the room, they were worried sick about Tiblou. So they sat opposite each other in the big chairs, saying nothing, waiting for news. It came at last around eleven o'clock and the relief on Annie's face told them it was good.

'Roger's treatment is working,' she announced. 'Tiblou is recovering fast and should, hopefully, be better soon. He's sleeping now... so I suggest you all do the same.'

Larna and Aron were too exhausted to go all the way upstairs to bed. They simply shut their eyes and fell asleep where they sat. As they drifted off, Larna murmured, 'Hope Tibs is really back in action tomorrow. We've got a lot to get ready and a long way to go. We really can't afford any more delays.'

* * *

Tibs came down early next morning, looking pale and moving stiffly as if he'd been punched and kicked all over.

'Are you going to be all right?' asked Violet.

'I think so,' he answered. 'As long as I continue taking Uncle Roger's potion.'

'A case of 'keep taking the tablets', eh?' joked Chet.

'I wish it was,' Tiblou said with a grimace. 'The mixture tastes like the juice of rotten Brussel sprouts and smells like Boggret.'

'Lovely!' commented Aron.

'Wimp!' teased Larna.

The rest of the morning was spent getting ready for their long journey to the Valley of Ice.

'Can't you just magic us there?' asked Larna. 'It would save a lot of time and trouble.'

'I'm afraid not. I haven't gained full adult wizard power, yet, which means I sometimes have to rely on my wits.' replied Tiblou. 'I can time-travel by transposing myself back to your era, as I've done twice recently, and I can travel very short distances like fading out of one room and appearing in another. But I can't go far. It takes away all my power and I'm left defenceless. Mordrog used to be able do it all the time, of course, and Edina can do it now. I've never understood why the forces of evil are always so much stronger than the forces of good.'

'So you have to travel with us?'

'I do.'

'Good!'

While Annie, Chet and Violet prepared the food and tents and other equipment that would be needed for a hike across difficult terrain, Larna and Aron went upstairs to help Tibs work on the dummy wand. In the library, there was a book containing the history of every magic wand that had ever existed in Sherwood. Mordrog's was there, right in the middle, with a large colour picture next to the description of all the evil things it could do.

'Now this is where my magic powers really come into their

58

own,' chuckled Tibs, placing his finger on the picture and then at the same spot on the wand. In a matter of moments, the dummy wand looked exactly like the wand in the book.

'Now we need to fire it up,' he said.

Larna and Aron stood back as the young wizard, who seemed to be getting back to his old self by the minute, wandered around, flexing his fingers at the wand and chanting a stream of strange words that neither of them understood. Then Tibs picked up the wand and handed it to Larna.

'Try it out,' he said.

Startled, 'Me?' she queried.

'Don't you want to? It won't bite!'

'I'm not sure to be honest, Tiblou. Yaya says the use of powers bring great responsibilities...'

'I'll do it!' exclaimed Aron, reaching for the wand.

'No!' commanded Tibs. 'Larna's older than you. She should be the one to do it.'

So, very gingerly, she took the wand and held it in her right hand.

'It's only loaded with light magic, so don't be scared, and anything that happens can immediately be reversed. So what would you like to do?'

'Conjure up a bowl of that exploding ice cream we had last time we were here.'

'Very well, then, see what happens,' Tiblou encouraged.

So Larna spoke her wish out loud as she waved the wand in a circle. *t*The ice cream appeared – but it was floating in the air!

'Look out, Aron!' she called, but it was too late. The dish tipped over and the ice cream went all over her brother's head.

'I'm sooooo sorry,' she cried, rushing forwards, but Aron put up his hand to stop her.

'You're not having any of this,' he told her, licking the brightly coloured creamy liquid, as it popped and fizzed down his face towards his mouth. 'It's mine!'

* * *

By mid-day, all the preparations were complete and, as they would be travelling to the Kingdom of Ice Aron and Larna borrowed a couple of winter jackets.

Annie insisted on everyone having something to eat – she said they didn't know when they would get another decent meal – and then everyone was ready to go. But as they pulled on hiking boots and hoisted their rucksacks onto their backs, Annie looked round for Ozzy.

'I want to instruct him to guard the castle,' she said. 'Violet's coming with us this time, so he'll be on his own. I want to show him where his food is and how to get in and out if he needs to. He's never been left on his own before.'

So everyone put their rucksacks down again and went looking for the tame Swooper. He was nowhere to be found. It was as if he'd disappeared off the face of the earth.

'We can't waste any more precious time looking for him. He'll be all right he knows his way around.' Said Chet.

So they shut up the castle and Tibs put a protective spell on it that would turn anyone who tried to break in into a weasel. With the exception of Ozzy. Leaving his pet Swooper weighed heavily on Tiblou's conscience, but they had to go immediately.

The party set off in single file, trudging silently along the paths between the ancient trees like climbers on the slope of Everest. Tiblou took the lead, followed by Annie, then Larna and Aron and finally Chet bring up the rear. Violet flew overhead, whizzing up and down the line chatting to everyone in turn and occasionally hitching a ride on someone's backpack when her wings grew tired. Everyone felt in good spirits, excited to be on their way to rescue Neve at last - except Chet. He started puffing and blowing and staggering about with every step they took.

'What's wrong with you?' asked Tiblou, turning round to stare at his brother's purple face. 'You're not usually like this. You're always the big strong one.'

'It's this bag,' puffed Chet, shifting the bulging rucksack around on his shoulders and wincing with discomfort. 'I swear it's three times the weight that it was when I packed it.'

A smile flickered around the corners of Tibs' mouth. 'Put it down a minute,' he said, holding up his hand to halt the rest of the line. The others gathered round to watch as their leader bent down to undo the straps. As he opened the flap, a single grey feather floated into the air and disappeared on the breeze. It was followed by an orange paddle beak and a pair of anxious-looking eyes.

'*Ozzy!*' exclaimed Tiblou. 'What on earth do you think you're playing at?'

Annie, who had most to do with the bird on a day-to-day basis, bent over and wagged her finger in the bird's face.

'You're very naughty to stow away like that,' she scolded, pointing back in the direction of the castle. 'Now go back home, get in through your flap and stay there until we come back.'

Ozzy didn't move.

'Go on!' she urged.

Still Ozzy didn't move.

'I'll say it one more time, Ozzy,' said Annie with a note of steel in her voice. 'Go back to Tiblou's,*t*

Reluctantly, the Swooper got to his feet and hung his head.

'He wants to come with us,' said Aron.

'Can't he come with us?' begged Larna.

'He'll slow us down,' grumbled Chet.

'And eat all our food,' added Annie.

'No, he won't,' argued Violet. 'He can fly along with me. What do you say, Tibs? You're the leader of this expedition.'

Tiblou looked at the sad face of his pet bird and at the hopeful faces of his two visitors.

'Of course he can come with us,' decided Tiblou with a smile. 'He might even be useful.'

'Softie!' murmured his mother as she brushed past him.

* * *

Having set out so late in the day, Larna did not expect to get far before they had to make camp for the night. So she was astonished when Chet pointed to some tall hills in the far distance and said that that was their destination for today.

'They're called The Hills of Amber Light,' explained Violet, who was hovering above their heads, and they're my favourite place in the whole of Sherwood. I was born there. The hills are my ancestral home.'

Larna opened her mouth to voice her amazement but closed it again immediately as everyone around her stopped and looked up at the sky. The sun was starting to set, turning the world to orange and gold.

'Here they come!' cried Chet, pointing to some distant specks on the horizon.

'Here *who* come?' asked Aron.

'You'll see,' Chet said with a smile.

Brother and sister looked at each other and shrugged their

shoulders. Something was going on and no doubt they would soon find out what it was.

The specks in the sky grew bigger and bigger as they gradually drew closer. They were white, that was the first thing Larna could see, and for a while she thought they must be giant birds of some kind. Then she saw they were horses...with wings.

'The Pegasii,' Tibs whispered in her ear. 'They're my special friends.'

The beautiful white horses with long flowing manes and delicate white wings circled overhead for a while like airliners stacking, waiting to land and then, one by one they touched down on the ground a short distance away. The first one, who was clearly the leader of the herd, then knelt down and gave a whiney that was clearly an invitation to approach.

'Come on, everyone,' called Tibs. 'Our transport awaits.'

The wizard led the way to the flying horses, pausing to stroke the leader gently on his nose and pat his gleaming white flank before climbing on his back. The others did the same, finding there was one Pegasii mount for each of them except for Ozzy who tucked himself inside Tiblou's coat and peeped out looking very happy. There was even a ride for Violet. Trailing the herd was a tiny foal with big eyes like a drawing in one of the storybooks Larna used to read when she was little. The fairy flew over and perched on her back with a whoop of joy.

'My little wings wouldn't have made it all that way!' she said.

At Tiblou's command, the line of horses took off into the air.

'Remember to hold tight,' he called over his shoulder. 'grasp the mane in front of you and grip with your knees. That's what they expect.'

It was wise advice because Aron, second in line, had never ridden before. So he almost fell off when his horse galloped forwards and suddenly lifted into the air. Larna was better prepared. She'd had some riding lessons when she was at Middle School and knew what to do.

'Serve you right for saying riding was sissy!' she shouted ahead to her brother.

Before long, the whole flight was airborne and the Pegasii wheeled round in a graceful arc as they headed for the hills. Soon everyone was high in the air where the wind was cold and their hair was blown back behind their ears. But the view was spectacular. Larna thought the fields looked like the old patchwork quilt her mother had given to a charity shop and the trees and buildings like the paintings on her bedroom wall at Neve's.

'*Yay!*' she shouted to express the exhilaration coursing through her veins.

Aron looked back at her and grinned. '*Yay!*' he echoed in agreement.

It didn't take long for the magnificent flying horses to reach the hills and Larna felt a pang of regret that this ride-of-a-lifetime would be over so soon. She had to remember they were on a vital expedition to save her grandmother's life, not an adventure holiday. As she dismounted from her steed she patted him gratefully on the flank. Then everyone waved goodbye, calling more thanks, as the Pegasii launched themselves into the air again and disappeared into the light of the setting sun. Sensing Larna and Aron's sadness, Annie clicked her fingers and beckoned to them urgently.

'Come on, you two,' she called. 'It's almost dark. There's work to be done. 'There was a small patch of grass to one side of the hill top and Annie chose that as their camping site.

Aron pulled a face and asked, 'Any chance of a small spell to help us with the tents, Tibs?'

'I would try, but I can't risk Edina locating our position and try one of her dirty tricks to slow us down.'

For the next half-an-hour nobody spoke as they struggled to unpack their belongings and put up their tents. When everything was done, Larna and Aron just wanted to crawl inside and go to sleep. The events of the last couple of days had been overwhelming and they knew there would be more demands on their strength and energy to come. But Violet wouldn't let them.

'You *must* come with me,' she insisted, leading them the short distance up the rocky path to the summit.

The three of them sat down on a boulder and stared at the sky. The moment the final fingernail of sun disappeared below the horizon, it was replaced by an almost full moon that rose vertically upwards like a helium balloon. It came to a stop right above their heads and, as if turned on by a switch, it began emitting amber light.

'So that's how the hills get their name,' whispered Larna.

Violet nodded, not wishing to spoil the moment by saying anything more. The three of them sat there, bathed in the warm amber light that made everything seem incredibly beautiful

CHAPTER THIRTEEN

ANNIE TO THE RESCUE

The following morning, everyone was up early and ready to go at first light. Another day closer to Neve and the expiry of Edina's ultimatum and the party were eager not to waste any more valuable time. So they struck camp and made their way down the winding hill path that led to a river at the bottom.

Because the rain fell every day in Upper Sherwood, the streams and rivers were always full and this one was no exception. As they reached it about an hour later, having enjoyed the downhill walk in the clear morning air, they found it presented a problem.

'There's no way across,' said Tibs. 'We'll have to make a bridge.'

'That'll take ages,' argued his brother. 'And there's not much wood nearby. We'll have to go a long way to find suitable materials.'

'It's a shame you can't just magic one up?' said Aron.

'I feel the same,' explained Tiblou.'

'Then we'll have to wade it,' said Larna.

'Don't think so, dear,' retorted Annie, pointing to the seething mass of white water flowing past at great speed. 'The current looks strong and it's bound to be very deep in the middle.'

'So what do we do?' wondered Violet, her wings glowing a reddish-purple in annoyance.

Aron's sharp eyesight solved the problem.

'Hey, what's this?' he called, racing down the bank and pointing to where the fast-flowing river was splashing and gurgling over some objects in the river. They were stepping stones. 'We can use these to get across, can't we?'

'If we're careful,' murmured Tibs.

The two teens opted to go first. Aron skipped across with great confidence, waiting on the opposite bank with Violet and Ozzy who had both flown across.

'Come on,' he called. 'It's easy.'

Larna didn't find it easy and took an age, balancing precariously on each stone before daring to step onto the next. But she made it at last, much to everyone's relief.

Tibs went next, Chet waiting behind so he could help Annie

to get across. The young wizard copied Aron's approach, skipping confidently from one stone to the other. But, right in the middle of the river, he lost his footing and almost fell in. Wobbling backwards and forwards, waving his arms about, he looked quite comical, but nobody laughed because of the seriousness of their situation. Instead, they all held their breath and willed him to regain his balance. He did at last, hurrying over the remaining stones and pitching forwards onto the opposite bank with a cry of relief. It wasn't very dignified, but nobody minded. He was safe.

That just left Annie and Chet. They could not possibly balance on the same stone together, so Chet followed his mother, watching carefully as she picked her way over the slippery footholds. They seemed to be crossing with ease until, right in the middle of the river, she suddenly turned sideways and threw herself into the raging torrent

'What are you doing, ma?' yelled Chet, plunging into the water after her. The others raced along the opposite bank, led by a frantic-looking Tiblou. The current carried Annie towards a distant bend and everyone watched in horror as she disappeared beneath the surface and did not come up again for a long time.

'I'll dive down and look for her!' yelled Chet.

'No need,' Tibs replied, pointing from the riverbank. 'There she is. She's okay!'

Annie was staggering out onto a tiny sandy beach, holding something triumphantly aloft in the air.

'What's she found?' asked Larna.

'She hasn't found anything,' replied Aron, his sharp eyes spotting what was in her hand. 'It's Mordrog's fake wand. It must have slipped out of Tibs' pocket when he wobbled about and nearly fell in. Annie spotted it and rescued it.'

As everyone ran to the dripping figure staggering up onto the bank, they saw what Aron said was true. Annie was indeed holding the all-important wand.

'Not much point in going any further without this,' she spluttered.

Tiblou and Chet gave their mother a hug, despite her soaking clothes.

'You're very brave, ma.' said Chet with a smirk.

'And very foolish,' added Tibs.

'Oh, be quiet, you two.' she scoffed. 'I'm as tough as an old boot despite my age...and size!'

Larna was worried that Annie and Chet might get pneumonia, having to stay in their wet clothes all day. And, as it was considered an emergency, Tibs took a huge risk. Waving his own wand, he created a swirling vortex of warm air like the one in the entrance to his castle. It encircled his mother and brother, drying them out like a personal spin drier. Soon they were back to normal again and continued on their way across the flat open plain that stretched out endlessly before them.

'That's today's crisis over and done with,' said Aron cheerfully. 'Should all be a piece of cake from now on.'

* * *

Deep in her ice palace, Edina was pacing around restlessly. Something was wrong, she could feel it in her witch's bones. Why had that strange coach appeared and almost succeeded in crushing some of her enemies to death? And the giant flowers at Blithe Cottage? She hadn't seen them attack Tiblou, but she'd heard how desperately ill their bites had made him afterwards. And why hadn't the coach and the flowers attacked Larna and Aron as well? It was as if someone was trying to isolate them for some reason. Whoever it was and for whatever reason, Edina didn't like it.

'I'm the power here,' she muttered to herself, shoving Selka out of her way so he rolled into the corner like a wet football. 'And *nobody* is going to stop me becoming ruler of Upper *and* Lower Sherwood.'

Just then, Rufus and Refina burst in. 'We're bored,' announced Rufus.

'Then why don't you read a book?' said Edina, indicating a bookshelf on the ice-wall full of books that were never opened. 'I used to love reading when I was your age.' She smiled fondly at the memory. 'Stories in which the Ogre finally succeeds in gobbling tup the Princess...the handsome prince dies a painful death at the hands of the trolls...the kindly old woodcutter is pecked to pieces by some killer crows...oh, yes! I used to love a story with a happy ending.'

The twins weren't listening.

'I know what you can do,' decided Edina, remembering her earlier anxieties and shoving them both through the entrance. 'Go and keep a look-out for me. I want to know if you see anyone or anything unusual. If you do, then come straight back here and report it.'

The twins wandered off, muttering and grumbling to themselves.

Once outside, Rufus and Refina crossed the ice bridge and climbed the nearest hill in order to get a good view of the surrounding frozen fields and trees. They had some fun grabbing their ankles and pulling each other back down the slope, but now they stood on the summit looking round at the empty, silent area.

'This is boring,' said the girl.

'I hate to say this but I agree with you, Fina,' said her twin. So he gave her a pinch that turned her arm bright blue.

'*Ouch!*' she yelled. 'I'll get you for that.'

Had they not been so busy inflicting the maximum amount of pain on each other, they would have noticed two shadowy figures entering their domain having travelled there via the Forest of Stone.

* * *

Aron had been right. The rest of the day passed off without any great drama or incident. The party walked steadily across the rocky terrain, sometimes in single file if the path between the tall grass was narrow, in groups if it was wider. Tibs was walking with Chet when they noticed Annie sitting down on a rock to rest for a while.

'That's the fifth time today she's done that,' commented Chet.

'Hardly surprising, is it?' replied his brother. 'She's no spring chicken and she's not exactly lightweight either. Besides, she took a real pasting in the coach and then in the river. I'm not surprised she's finding this hard.'

'I just hope she doesn't slow us down too much,' murmured Chet. 'A chain is only as strong as its weakest link and all that.'

'Don't let her hear you saying that,' hissed Tibs. 'Our lives won't be worth living if she thinks we consider her weak.'

They went on and on, but there was nothing to see of any interest or excitement. Larna and Aron trudged on side by side, heads down, feet aching.

'This is turning out to be some relaxing holiday,' said Aron sarcastically.

'Don't want to talk,' returned his sister. 'Saving my energy.' In fact, Larna was preoccupied with thinking about Cai. For some reason she couldn't understand, she sensed he was near and that made her want to meet him again. It was a feeling that stayed with her and wouldn't go away.

Just before sundown, as they were looking for another suitable campsite, Ozzy suddenly became agitated.

'What is it, my friend?' asked Tiblou, ruffling the downy feathers on the back of his pet's neck. Ozzy pointed his orange beak to the east and let out an urgent squawk. Everyone turned in that direction and saw a flock of birds in the far distance, circling in the sky and then dropping down like dive-bombers to feed on some creature they'd savagely killed.

'Swoopers,' whispered Violet, a shudder of fear running through her delicate body. 'They attacked me once. I was lucky to get away with my life.'

'I think we're safe,' announced Tibs. 'They haven't spotted us and they're too busy feeding anyway. But we must keep our eyes open for them from now on. They're deadly killers and they appear out of nowhere when you least expect them. Thanks for the warning, Ozzy.'

Once camp had been made and sandwiches eaten, Larna slipped away to her tent. She was tired and preoccupied by her thoughts. She snuggled down into her sleeping bag and let herself drift away. Then Cai appeared, standing beside her looking just as she remembered.

'I've come because you were thinking of me, and may need my help to find your grandmother, the white witch, Neve.' he said gruffly.

Larna sat up and reached out to him...but he wasn't there! Had she been dreaming or had the Undine Prince really come to see her? She didn't know. You could never tell in this magical, topsy-turvy world of future Sherwood. It didn't matter. Larna lay back down feeling peaceful and happy. She was convinced Cai was waiting for her somewhere nearby.

CHAPTER FOURTEEN

ALL HOPE AND NO HOPE

Larna could not sleep. She tossed and turned, her body tired but her mind hyperactive, imagining what dangers may lay ahead. Eventually she dropped off for a while in the small hours of the morning, but she was awake again before dawn...and knew what she had to do.

Quietly, she sneaked out of her tent and did up the flap again so nobody would discover she was gone until it was too late. The first fingers of light signalling the new day were just appearing over the horizon as she tiptoed away from the sleeping camp and made her way towards a large outcrop of rock that stood above the flat plain like a building. Why she was heading in this direction, she did not know. But something was telling her to go this way. If she did, she believed she would find Cai.

The morning sun was up, but not strong enough to warm the air as Larna reached the rock. She walked all round it, her heart sinking as she saw nothing out of the ordinary that would explain why she'd been drawn here. She knew the others would be up by now and, any moment, her absence would be noted. So she was about to head back, making the (half-truthful) excuse that she couldn't sleep and had gone for a walk to clear her head, when she noticed the crevice in the rock. It wasn't very wide – just enough to squeeze through – but it was unmistakably an entrance. To what? She didn't know... but she knew she had to find out.

Drawing a deep breath to make herself as thin as possible and praying she wouldn't get stuck, she squeezed herself into the narrow crack and wriggled her way through.

She didn't notice that a charm on her bracelet had snagged on a stone and broke the clasp.

Larna found herself in a dimly-lit cavern, looking down a gigantic stone staircase. It wound round and round, down and down, until it disappeared into the darkness below.

'This must be an entrance to the underworld,' she said to herself, her voice echoing all around in the cavernous space. Without another moment's hesitation, she started to make her way down the steps. She knew this was the right thing to do. Cai must have drawn her to this place to show her how to return underground.

'Sure beats falling through a hole in the ground,' she murmured. The descending steps went on and on and the back of her legs began to ache as she plodded further down. Just to be on the safe side, she took out her mobile phone and tried to text Aron where she was and what she intended to do, but it slipped out of her hands and fell clonk clonk clonk on each step, away into the darkness.

'Oh damn, now what!' she muttered, rubbing the back of her aching legs. The dull pain reminded her of a family holiday to Egypt when she and Aron climbed up a huge pyramid and both of them were almost crippled the next day. But she couldn't give up now. It would be even more painful to turn round and climb all the way up again. The die was cast. She had to go on.

Eventually, the darkness started to give way to some light and her spirits lifted at the thought of completing this endless downward journey. Then, with a sigh of relief, she turned the last spiral and stood in the big empty cave, her legs weak and wobbly, her heart fluttering. Where was the light coming from? She looked up and saw the ceiling covered with Lumins, the tiny creatures that gave out light. This was a good sign. They were friendly and had helped her when she was underground before.

Now the question was which way to go? There were many possibilities. Passages led where they led. Then Larna remembered the Undines were water-creatures and King Drisco, Cai's father, had appeared out of a lake when he came to thank her for rescuing his son. So she knew that was what she should head for. Methodically, one by one, she stood at the beginning of each passage and listened intently. But they gave no clue they led to water...that is until she reached the last-but-one. Straining to hear with absolute focus, she was sure she could detect a gushing sound in the far distance. This must be it! A stream or waterfall that fed the vast underground lake. She only had to follow it to reach her destination.

Her heart fluttering at the thought of running into Cai around the next bend. Larna made her way along beside the narrow stream that flowed between the increasingly slimy rocks. Whenever the way grew dark, the Lumins above would shine more brightly to illuminate her path.

'Thanks, my friends,' she called, looking up and giving them a thumbs-up sign. Eventually, the path grew wider and the sound of water became louder. Turning a final corner past an outcrop of moss-

70

covered rock, she found herself at a lake. She had made it!

'Cai!' she called. 'Are you there?' There was no answer.

'Are you there, King Drisco?' she tried again. 'It's me, Larna Gorry. You saved me from the crazy Boggrets.'

The silence was deafening. Suddenly, fear clutched at Larna's heart. Maybe she'd made a terrible mistake by coming down here. She was alone and defenceless and there seemed to be no sign of her friends. What was she going to do now? She wasn't sure she had the strength to go all the way back up, even if she could find the way.

Feeling angry with herself for being so foolish, she was about to yell in frustration when she thought she saw Cai coming towards her. He looked much bigger than when he'd appeared to her the previous night, his features looked coarser and his expression stern, but it was undoubtedly him.

'Cai!' she exclaimed, waiting for an embrace. Larna closed her eyes as she felt two arms encircle her waist, but his grip was rough and a familiar stench filled her nostrils, as the being morphed back to his natural state. Her eyes snapped open and she saw a grotesque face grinning triumphantly up at her.

'You're not Cai.' she stammered, fear clutching at her insides like a stomach ache.

'No, I'm not,' scoffed a deep gravelly voice.

'Then who are you?'

'I'm King Killian, Lord of the Boggrets.' He said, puffing out his chest with pride.

Moments later, two Boggret guards appeared and roughly tied ropes round Larna's wrists, then dragged her along behind the king like a captured animal.

'What do you want with me, Killian?' called Larna, bravely. 'I'm no use to you.'

'On the contrary,' sneered the fearsome ruler, turning round to grin at her delightedly.

'I'm so glad I heard you calling out to your lover boy. It gave me the opportunity to do a little shape-shifting of my own, a skill I haven't practiced for many years. And my reward is a new personal slave. My others are getting old and tired and will have to be disposed of soon. You will make an admirable replacement.'

Larna's blood ran cold. 'How long do you intend to keep me?' she demanded.

'Why, for the rest of your life.' he answered.

Larna had never felt so terrified or so alone as she did being dragged along by the leering Boggret guards. Nobody would ever find her because no one knew where she was. She felt totally without hope. But, had she been able to look up, she would have seen the pattern of lights on the high ceiling had changed. The steady points of light provided by the Lumins had disappeared and been replaced by gentle pulses that were sending out an urgent signal.

CHAPTER FIFTEEN

DEATH FROM THE SKY

Back above ground, there was great con sternation at the camp when it was discovered that Larna was missing. Aron had called her several times, so it came as a great shock to everyone when he eventually opened her tent flap and found she wasn't there.

'Where is she?' wondered Annie. 'There's nothing of interest round here.'

'Maybe Edina's taken her?' suggested Violet.

'Why would she do that?' queried Tiblou. 'What she's after is here inside my pocket. No, I don't think it's anything to do with her.'

'Who then?' wondered Chet.

'Maybe nobody,' suggested Aron, perceptively. 'She could have wandered off in search of her Undine friend.'

'We'll just have to wait and see if she comes back then,' sighed Annie.

'We haven't got the time, Ma,' protested Chet.

'We can't go on without her, either,' said Tibs, grimly.

So they waited for half-an-hour, growing increasingly impatient with each passing minute.

'This is ridiculous!' cried Aron, jumping to his feet. 'Why don't we go and look for her?

'Good idea,' agreed Chet. 'Let's all fan out and head in different directions. We can cover everywhere like that.'

'I'll stay here with Ozzy,' Annie suggested. 'In case she comes back when you're all away. What about you, Violet?'

'I can fly up and down like an eye-in-the-sky.'

An hour-or-so later, everyone returned feeling tired and dejected. Annie produced a packet of elderberry tea and emptied it into a large concertina camping mug. And, using the last of her drinking water, she poured it into the mug.

'There's no sign of her anywhere,' sighed Chet, flopping down on a fallen log they were using as a seat. 'If she's gone walk-about it's very inconsiderate of her.'

'Let's just double-check we covered everywhere,' said Tibs, 'I searched all the open grassland over to the east.' Taking his turn for a few sips of the tea then passed the mug on.

'I did the same to the west,' said his brother.

'I went all the way down the long path that leads to that outcrop of rock over there,' explained Aron, pointing into the distance. 'There was no sign of her.'

'What about you, Violet?' asked Tiblou. 'You had the best view of everyone.'

Before the fairy could answer, Ozzy emitted a loud squawk.

'Quiet, Ozzy!' Shushed Annie.

'I flew over everywhere,' reported Violet, her wings looking blue with fatigue. 'But I didn't see anything either – no movement, no footprints, no clues. Where Larna has gone is a complete mystery...'

At this point, Ozzy gave another squawk and started pecking at Tiblou's foot.

'*Ozzy!*' scolded Annie. 'I told you not...'

'Hang on a minute, mum,' said Tibs quietly. 'Ozzy doesn't usually make a fuss. He's trying to tell us something.' The wizard bent down and stroked his beloved pet under its beak. 'What is it, Oz?'

Ozzy rolled his eyes and pointed his beak at the sky. The others followed his gaze and felt their stomachs contracting in horror. Circling silently above their heads were the Swoopers.

'Get under cover!' yelled Tibs. '*Hide. **Now!**'*

Nobody needed telling twice. As the huge killer birds peeled off and began their dive, the group fled in all directions. Believing his mother was right behind him, Tiblou made for a nearby bush, diving underneath the dense foliage. It made a perfect hiding place. Chet had the same idea and squeezed in beside his brother, parting the leaves above his head to see what was going on.

The wild Swoopers were the size of geese. They were dirty grey with the same huge orange beak as Ozzy, only theirs tapered over at the end into a sharp point. Their bulbous eyes were a piercing and, as they dived, they spun round like drills emitting terrifying ear-splitting shrieks. Seeing one of the killers heading straight for them, Chet dropped back and copied his brother who was crouching down with his hands over his head as if waiting for a bomb to go off. The Swooper skimmed over their heads, taking some of the foliage with it, and shot back into the air with a scream of fury.

'Stay where you are, Chet,' whispered Tibs urgently. 'He'll be back again in a minute. They want their breakfast and we're the main course.'

Over in the camp, Annie had chosen to shelter in Larna's tent that still hadn't been taken down. She couldn't run far or very fast, so it seemed the only option. At least she would be hidden from view and maybe the birds wouldn't see her. But it was a vain hope. Another Swooper spotted her crawling under the canvas and made her the target of its attack. With an extra-loud piercing squeal, the creature spun down towards her and ripped the tent to shreds as it powered up out of its dive. Annie was left exposed like an animal, crouching down and looking up at the sky in silent terror as she waited for the next killer dive. Luckily, Violet spotted her predicament and flew over to help.

'This may not work,' she shouted above the screaming of the birds, 'but it's worth a try.' She took out her tiny wand and cast a spell at the returning Swooper. It stung the killer as it descended, making it swerve aside from its second attack on Annie. But the bird was angry and, as it shot upwards again, it knocked Violet aside with its wing. The tiny fairy, no match for the powerful Swooper, was knocked to the ground where she lay motionless, perfect prey for another attack. Annie ran to pick up Violet and hurried across to bushes at the edge of the campsite. They didn't offer much cover, but they were better than nothing. At least the thin branches would make it more difficult for the birds to peck at her directly.

Aron was in the worst predicament of all. Searching around desperately, he had not been able to find adequate cover and so had decided to flee. It was a foolish decision based on nothing more than panic and fear. Unlike the others, who had some kind of protection from above, he was out in the open and completely vulnerable to attack. Sensing this, two further Swoopers decided to pursue him, taking it in turns to dive down and peck at him mercilessly.

Larna was right, he thought to himself as he willed his unfit legs to run faster, *I have spent too much time playing computer games.* The boy found himself racing back along the path he had followed earlier. His only hope of survival was to reach the big outcrop of rock in the distance, but he didn't think he would make it. Screaming like a banshee, the first Swooper zoomed overhead and only by throwing himself to the ground did he avoid his face being bitten. As he scrambled to his feet again, the second bird came at him in level flight, knocking him to the ground again and taking a painful bite out of his arm. He got himself up and, pressing one hand to stem the flow of blood, staggered on, pushing himself to the limit to try and reach the safety of the rocks. He saw the birds circling above, waiting for their final dive. Now he knew what it felt like to be on the receiving end of such attacks. It was terrifying.

The attack had now reached crisis point. The leaves of the bushes had been ripped away leaving Tibs and Chet totally exposed. Annie was still crouched down under the trees on the other side of the camp quaking with fear as she protected Violet and waited for the first agonising stab in her back.

Meanwhile, Aron blundered on, weaving, ducking and diving as the Swoopers took turns to spiral down and peck at him. Safety in the shelter under the rocks never seemed to get any nearer.

Suddenly, there was an unholy cry different from the aggressive screaming of the angry Swoopers as they dived on their prey. It was a long high-pitched howling threatening danger. It echoed off the rocks like an alarm call and the Swoopers reacted to it immediately. They cut short their attacks and regrouped above the devastation of the camp, flying in a circle as they had done when they were first spotted.

'What the hell was that?' gasped Chet, daring to look up for the first time.

'Who knows?' replied Tibs, stumbling to his feet. 'But whatever it was seems to have called those beasts off.'

A further cry, louder and more menacing than the previous one filled the morning air and they saw Ozzy launching himself into the air towards the other Swoopers.

'It's Ozzy!' shouted Annie, hurrying over to join her sons with the stunned figure of Violet in her arms. 'He must know the Swoopers' warning-cry and has used it to deflect them.'

'You're right, Ma!' exclaimed Chet, pointing to the sky where the birds had started to follow Ozzy as he led them away from the camp. 'They think he's spotted some kind of danger and are following him to safety.'

'I hate to think what'll happen to him when they find out it's a false alarm and they've been cheated out of their big meal,' murmured Tibs, a suspicion of tears in his eyes at the thought of never seeing his playful companion again.

Over at the rock, the two Swoopers pursuing Aron were the last to respond to the call. With the shelter of a narrow crevice tantalisingly in view, Aron had been knocked to the ground by his two attackers. Covering his head with his hands, he made himself as small as possible and tried to stop them pecking at his eyes. Suddenly, when all seemed lost, the twin tormentors left him alone and took off into the air with squawks of anger and frustration. Their wings whirring, they sped off to join the others who were now disappearing into the distance behind Ozzy. Hardly able to believe his luck, Aron clambered to his feet and staggered the last few metres to the rock, squeezing himself through the narrow gap and collapsing onto the floor of the hall-like cavern inside. And there he stayed, relieved and exhausted, scarcely able to believe he was still alive.

With the Swoopers gone, an eerie silence returned to the plains. The others gathered up their belongings and prepared to move on.

'Everyone OK?' asked Tibs. When the others nodded, including Violet who had recovered from her ordeal and seemed none the worse for it, the wizard added, 'Let's get going then. The last thing we want is for the Swoopers to twig what Ozzy has done and come back looking for us again. We can't afford to dawdle, even though Larna is missing.'

'Where's Aron?' asked Chet, anxiously. 'Don't say we've lost him too.'

'He's at the big rock over there,' answered Annie. 'I saw him squeeze inside when two Swoopers chased him. I expect he's recovering. We can pick him up as we go past. The Forest of Stone is our next landmark and we have to pass that way to get there.' So,

feeling very relieved to be safe and on the move again, the hikers made their way down the path that Aron and his sister had taken.

Meanwhile, inside the cavern, Aron was just getting to his feet and planning to return to his friends when he spotted something on the ground. Stooping to pick it up, he gasped in amazement and almost dropped it as if he'd had an electric shock.

'Larna's gold bracelet.' He whispered, staring at it with mixed emotions of joy and alarm. His sister must have come this way and dropped it when she squeezed through the narrow gap. But, where was she? In the dim light from the entrance Aron spotted the top of a mighty stone staircase leading down to the underworld.

'Larna, you *idiot!*' he shouted, his cry echoing round the cave like a thousand voices. Now, Aron understood what his sister had done. Could she have returned below ground in search of Cai! So what should he do now? Should he go and tell the others where she'd gone or follow her to bring her back? His head said one thing but his heart said the other. Without a moment's thought he headed for the steps. Aron had been told enough about the underworld to know Larna had placed herself in terrible danger by returning underground and his first instinct was to go and bring her back. So he took the stairs at a gallop, going down and down, round and round, just like his sister had done.

By the time the others reached the outcrop of rock, he was deep underground.

'*Aron!*' they called together, expecting him to appear at any moment. When he didn't, they split up and walked round the big rock in opposite directions. 'We know you're here, Aron,' shouted Tiblou. 'Come on out, we need to move on ... ***ARON!***'

'It's no use, Tibs,' sighed Chet, his shoulders dropping wearily. 'He's not here.'

'Then where is he?' queried Annie.

'Where are they both?' mused Tibs.

'Shall I fly in through that fissure?' suggested Violet. 'There might be some clue as to where they've gone inside.'

The wizard shook his head. 'We can't waste any more time on this,' he decided, looking up at the sun which was high in the sky. 'It's midday already and we won't reach Edina if we don't keep going.'

'But we can't just abandon them!' cried Annie, horrified.

'I'm not suggesting that, mum,' answered Tibs coolly. 'Chet, you stay here and continue to search for them. I'll journey on to our rendezvous with Violet and mom. That way we can solve both problems – find the missing teens and deliver the wand to Edina.'

'Will you be able to handle her on your own?' asked Chet anxiously.

'I'm not planning to hang around for long,' replied his brother. 'We give her the wand and get going with Neve. That's the only way this plan is going to work.'

So, with heavy hearts, the three remaining travellers set off on their mission, leaving Chet on his own at the rock.

'And don't try squeezing through that crevice to see what's inside,' called Annie, turning back and waving. 'You're too big and you'll get stuck.'

'Don't worry, Ma, I won't,' chuckled Chet. 'I'm sure the answer to their disappearance isn't inside there, anyway.'

CHAPTER SIXTEEN

LOST AND FOUND

Larna decided resistance was futile and trudged along behind her two Boggret guards to stop them jerking their ropes in such a painful manner. Not that this deterred them. Every now and then one of them would turn and, with a gleeful leer yank the rope the creature was holding so that Larna fell forwards or was stretched by the other rope. Then the two of them laughed heartily, a high-pitched shriek that echoed round the underground passages and caves through which they were travelling. Larna's only relief was when Killian, striding ahead of his servants, grew annoyed at the noise and stopped to cuff them both round the head with the back of his hand. Then they ceased their game...for a while.

As they travelled, Larna caught a terrible whiff of her captors marching ahead of her. She fought the impulse to gag, fearing it would be insulting and provide an excuse for them to torment her further. But as the tunnels widened and noise could be heard in the distance - a low hubbub, like a huge growling animal - the stench grew stronger and Larna was forced to breathe through her mouth to avoid being sick. She remembered this smell from her previous visit to the underworld. It was clear the Boggrets never ever washed and the stink of their bodies was overwhelming. It hung in the air and stuck to her like an invisible glue. Her face and hands felt sticky with it already. She longed to wash herself, to scrub it off and breathe fresh air again. But she realized this was not going to happen probably for a very long time, if ever. She just hoped she would get used to the appalling smell. She knew you can get used to anything in the end.

Cai had told her about the Boggrets before. Originally they had lived in Upper Sherwood where they had persecuted Cai's people, the Undines, who lived peacefully in the lakes and streams. Eventually, one of Cai's ancestors decided enough was enough and, took his people deep underground to escape their tormentors. The plan worked and for many years the Undines lived in peace again, occupying all the underground lakes and streams in Lower Sherwood. But, one sad day, they were spotted and their secret refuge exposed. The Boggrets began coming down to hunt them for sport and, liking the darkness and the barren rock of the underworld, they decided to move below ground as well. Ever since then, the two races have lived in uneasy opposition, the Boggrets, afraid of water, dominated the land areas and the Undines keeping themselves to themselves in the water. But Cai had said with a sigh that it was always something of an unequal contest. The Boggrets were strong and ruthlessly cruel; the Undines gentle, loving and kind. Eventually, King Killian would achieve his ambition of wiping out the Undines and taking control of the whole underworld – unless the young prince and his elderly father could stop them with the help of their brave people.

As the stench in the air became unbearable, King Killian stopped and breathed it in with relish like a hiker who has reached a hilltop taking in the bracing breeze.

'Aah, the smell of home!' he announced with satisfaction. Then he turned to Larna with a leer. 'Come, human. Come and see where you'll live for the rest of your days.' He snorted.

They emerged from a final tunnel into a huge cave containing hundreds of small buildings carved into the rock, each with a single rounded entrance at the front. As they approached, more Boggrets emerged from these cramped homes and stood lining the way as the King passed.

Larna noticed they looked smaller and thinner than the two guards escorting her. But, big or small, they all had the same greeny-grey wart-covered skin, bulging eyes that made them look like trolls. *Yes, that's what they remind me of,* Larna thought. *Trolls from children's stories. But these are real – horribly real and stinky.* At Killian's approach, the Boggrets began to cheer and, at the same time, pelt his prisoner with anything they could lay their hands on. Larna felt herself being hit by flying stones, rotting vegetables and old bones. One of the latter bounced off the side of her head, causing blood to flow down her face.

'*Enough!*' roared the King. 'My new slave shall remain unharmed.'

Instantly, the crowd stood silent. Larna got the feeling they were terrified of their ruler and did exactly what he said for fear of retribution.

The sea of caves dwellings gave way to a small hill on which stood a grander stone building. Killian's. It had a huge wooden front door with more Boggret guards standing either side holding wicked-looking wooden spears with pointed ends. The rest of the building appeared to have few windows and a chimney that ran up the right-hand side had smoke coming out of the top and disappearing high up to the roof. For a moment Larna watched, fascinated, as the billowing puffs twisted upwards through a narrow vent towards a speck of light at the top. *That's the upper world,* thought Larna, tears gushing from her eyes as she realized everything she had left behind – safety, her family, her friends and her freedom, all for her ridiculous and unsuccessful search for Cai. But she was not allowed to weep for long. A sharp prod from one of the Boggrets sent her stumbling forwards towards the ugly stone structure. The guards at the door saluted and stood back as the King swept inside followed by his tired, sickened and very frightened captive.

* * *

Larna was put to work right away. She was taken into a small circular courtyard and shown some piles of logs stacked up all round the walls.

'You shall be my fire slave,' announced the King, handing her a small axe. 'It is your job - no, it is your *duty* – to chop these logs, brought down from above, into smaller ones and stack them by my fire.'

Larna looked at the huge logs and the tiny axe in horror. 'But I c-can't possibly...' she began.

Leaning closer, Killian cut her short, 'You can and you will!' he hissed, his stinking breath rising up into her face. 'My fire must never go out. Indeed, it must never even die down. I like it blazing night and day, do you understand?' Larna nodded.

'Answer me when I speak to you!' shouted the King, raising his hand to strike Larna's face but changing his mind at the last minute. An injured slave was no use to him, but a terrified one was.

'Y-yes,' stammered Larna.

'Yes, what?' repeated the King, his eyes blazing with fury.

It took Larna a moment or two to appreciate what he meant.

'Yes, King Killian,' she said.

Watched by a Boggret guard, Larna spent the rest of the day struggling with the logs. The wood was hard and the axe was blunt, but she found the wood split easily lengthways and, by selecting the smallest logs from the stack, she was able to produce a reasonable amount of suitable logs for the fire. The watching guard prodded her with his pointed stake and indicated she should pick them up. Her hands already blistered and bleeding from using the axe, the exhausted teenager endured cuts and splinters as she picked up the largest armful of logs she could carry and staggered with them towards a door indicated by the guard. She stumbled through, almost dropping them as her feet went from hard stone to soft animal skin rug, and she deposited her load in a huge basket beside a roaring fire.

As she left the room, she took a quick look round. This was obviously King Killian's personal quarters and they contrasted sharply with everything else she had seen before. The danced with bright yellow light from the fire and was warm to the point of being hot. There was a large window partially covered with a tatty ancient tapestry. A throne-like chair beside the fire was piled with cushions. A table in the corner was stacked with food. Roast meat, bread piled in a heap and bowls of appetising fruit and nuts in abundance. She wondered where on earth, or under it, the Boggrets had got the food from. Realising she hadn't eaten since the day before, Larna felt herself being drawn towards this inviting spread, but a sharp poke from the guard's stick sent her scurrying back towards the door to fetch more of the logs. It was clear Killian used his position as all-powerful ruler to make life as comfortable for himself as possible. His people in the hovels outside looked thin, hungry and cold. By contrast, the home of their ruler seemed to them to be the last word in comfort and luxury.

By the end of the day, Larna was on the point of collapse when the King appeared, snapped his fingers at the guard and disappeared into his inner sanctum, slamming the door behind him. The guard prodded Larna once again and led her down some narrow stone steps to a tiny windowless room with a single large loaf of bread and a stone pitcher of water in the corner. The bread was stale, rock hard, and the water had bits floating in it that Larna didn't care to think about, but she began eating and drinking ravenously, eager to fill her aching stomach and sooth her sandpaper dry throat.

Out of the dark a timid voice said, 'Leave some for us,'

Larna screamed, dropped the food and scrambled backwards until she hit the wall.

'Don't be frightened, we aren't going to hurt you,' croaked a female voice. 'We are Boggret slaves too.'

Squinting into the darkness, Larna saw movement. 'Who *are* you?' She gasped. She could just make out two skeletal figures crouching in the far corner. They were covered in dark matted hair and looked like a pair of ferocious animals. Her heart rate immediately shot up again.

'*What* are you?' she asked, flattening herself to the wall. In panic, she wondered if this nightmare of a day would ever end.

'It's alright, it's alright,' soothed the first voice.

As Larna's eyes became more accustomed to the darkness she saw two figures shuffle towards her on their knees, hands held out, palms up in the universal gesture of peace. They had dog-like ears and short snouts like Tiblou used to have. That was before Larna and Aron's blood, serum extract and DNA helped reverse the mutating race back into human form. That was on their first sojourn into the Sherwood forest of the future, fifteen months ago. In that instant, Larna knew who they were.

'*Oh. My. God.* You're Zebedia Gorry aren't you?' she said as relief coursed through her body. 'And you must be June.' She whispered to the slight figure, struggling to get to her feet.

Shell shocked, the woman said, 'Yes.' And tentatively stretched out her hand to stroke Larna's arm, then cheek. 'What's happened to you? Why are you still so...smooth?'

Larna saw the absurdity of the situation and suddenly broke into a fit of hysterical giggles because they looked like a pair of scruffy Chewbaccas in rags from Star Wars. Shaking her head, she thought, 'Oh boy, this is going to take some explaining.'

Zebedia, who had been sitting quietly while this exchange had been going on said, 'It hardly seems right to say welcome to this hellhole of a place, but neither of us can deny that we are very pleased to see another human being.' He gave a deep chesty cough. 'We are at a disadvantage here, though, you obviously know who *we* are, but, *who are you?*'

'Oh my lord, this will come as a massive shock to you both ...I'm Larna, Larna Gorry,' she paused, 'from your distant past, in the twenty-first century.' She looked from one to the other for their reaction. Then dropped the final bombshell. '*And*, I believe that we are very, **very** distantly related.'

* * *

Larna was glad she hadn't wolfed very much of the paltry amount of food that had been left in the cell for them. Sitting cross legged on the cold stone floor, they softened the bread by dipping it into the fetid water, which, Larna was assured, hadn't hurt Zeb and June in all the years they had been incarcerated.

'Now, tell us about yourself, and how you came to be in our world.' Said Annie's long lost husband, coughing.

It wasn't easy recounting what had happened to everyone in Larna's century, Zebedia's time line, and right up until she was captured by the Boggrets. But, she gave it a shot and hoped for the best. She didn't have the heart to tell them about the death of Balgaire. If they ever managed to escape from the Boggrets back to upper Sherwood, then would be the time and, no doubt Tiblou would do the honours.

'So,' said June, 'You got into your current predicament in pursuit of your underwater friend, Cai.'

Larna nodded, hanging her head with shame at her utter stupidity. All of a sudden she felt weary to the bone and just wanted to curl up and sleep. But June leaned forward and raised the girl's head by putting a furry finger under her chin.

'Don't be so hard on yourself, you aren't the only one who followed a dream and ended up in this dire place you know. I went to meet my beau one sunny afternoon, fell through the ground into under Sherwood and the clutches of the Boggrets. When Zeb came looking for me he was captured too. We've been their slaves too many years to remember, gave up hope long ago and became resigned to dyeing down here.' June heaved a shuddering sigh. 'The Boggrets call this place Tophet, which is very apt because loosely translated it means, hell.'

Choked with emotion, Larna changed the subject. 'Cai's father gave me a disk for saving his son's life. Annie fainted when she saw it. It was when you left to find June. So, I do know a bit about the two of you. It also showed how you were captured by the Boggrets ... It was all on the disk...' She trailed off.

Zeb sensed Larna's distress and the conversation changed tack once again. 'So, Larna Gorry, you say that there is some of this reversing serum left.' He had a coughing fit.

'That's correct,' Larna told him, nodding enthusiastically. 'Tiblou kept some back in case we'd missed anyone who wanted to become human again.'

'There's hope for us yet, then,' Zeb said, rubbing one of his canine ears and smiling broadly.

'You're forgetting one thing,' sighed June, patting him patiently on the arm. 'We have to get out of here first.'

That night, curled up on a bed of old smelly rags like an animal in one of the corners, Larna found Cai's image appearing in front of her again. He seemed to smile at her in an encouraging way, she sighed and her anger, already weakened by June's kind words, melted away like frost in the sunshine. His smile seemed to promise that everything would be all right. She certainly hoped so. They couldn't get much worse than they were at this moment. Could they?

CHAPTER SEVENTEEN

THE FOREST OF STONE

Tiblou, Annie and Violet had not continued far on their journey before the fears the young wizard had discussed with his brother began to come true. Annie found it hard to keep up with her companions, often lagging behind and needing to sit down from time to time to rest. On one occasion, she took off her shoes to ease her aching feet.

'Sorry about this,' she said, rubbing her toes. 'Wouldn't do it in front of anyone else.'

Before long it became clear that Annie might have to be left behind if they were to reach Edina in time. But the idea was problem leaving him on his own. But not Annie. She would be very vulnerable and, besides, she was their mother and needed protecting at all times.

Sensing his brother's anxiety about Annie's ever slowing progress, Chet asked, 'Isn't there a spell you could use to help ma?'

Tibs shook his head. 'I'm not sure...'

'Maybe I can help,' said Violet. Without another word, the tiny fairy flew over to the bag containing their remaining food supply and took out a bag of apples. Grunting with the effort of lifting them into the air, she flew off with them towards a line of trees on the outskirts of the Stone Forest.

'Hey! What are you doing, Violet?' called Annie, crossly. 'Supplies are dangerously low as it is. We can't afford to waste any food.'

'You'll see,' was all their little companion would say.

Carefully placing the apples on the ground, Violet flew up and perched on one of the branches, waiting. Tiblou grew impatient, watching from a distance and repeatedly pointing up at the sun to indicate time was passing. Violet just shook her head and ignored him. Just as the wizard was about to give up and march on, there was a movement amongst the trees. A flash of grey. Then an animal appeared, eating the apples and coming closer. It was about the size of a donkey with a shaggy coat and a strong back. Violet flew down and whispered in the creature's ear. It recoiled, baying loudly and shaking its furry head. But she persisted in a pleading manner and eventually it stood there waiting. Violet flew back across to her companions.

'The animal of the Stone Forest is prepared to carry Annie as far as the Valley of Ice in return for being fed.' she announced.

'We don't have enough.' began Annie, but Tibs interrupted her.

'We'll find some along the way,' he said. 'Tell the creature that we accept his kind offer and we're grateful he's prepared to assist us on our journey.'

And so, perching on the back of the donkey-like creature she immediately named it Furgal and, looking like an illustration from a Medieval manuscript, Annie continued on her way in relative comfort.

* * *

Annie's anxiety about rewarding her patient mount seemed to have been allayed as they stopped beside a fast flowing stream inside the Forest of Stone. One of the trees appeared to be an apple tree. Annie stretched up and picked one intending to lean forward and feed Furgal, but it felt unusually heavy and when she tried to nibble it herself, she found it was made of stone!

'Good job I didn't take a big bite,' she said ruefully. 'Would have broken my teeth.'

'Problem solved,' called Violet pointing her wand at another tree growing in the shadow of the stone one. Apples appearing on its branches looked crisp, juicy and edible. The travellers feasted on them, gave a huge handful to the animal and then filled their bags with as many as they could carry for the journey ahead.

The further they traversed into the forest, the fewer living trees they found. Before long, there was nothing but stone trees with solid stone trunks like pillars in a cathedral and stone branches that hung over their head like grey unmoving arms. The atmosphere was claustrophobic. At any moment they expected one of the heavy branches to come crashing down on their heads and crush them to death.

'How much further through this desolate place?' Annie moaned.

'I'm not sure,' answered Tiblou, 'If there's a clearing soon, we can rest there'

It was so gloomy in the petrified forest it was difficult to tell whether it was night or day. So Violet flew up high amongst the trees to take a look at the sky and came down to report that the sun was setting.

'Then we'll have to stay the night.' decided Tibs, 'and move on as fast as we can before first light.'

Tibs fingers circled the air and a stone twig broke off a tree and drew a rough map in the dirt. 'According to this and the speed we're travelling; we should come to a short barren plain leading to the Valley of Ice by tomorrow afternoon.'

Annie patted Furgal's flank. 'Now I have my trusty steed we'll get there a bit faster, provided nothing else delays us.'

In the first clearing they prepared to stay the night. There was no wood to build a fire and so they sat around, drank sparingly of their water between eating a supper of apples and broken biscuits, then curling up in their sleeping bags ready for the early start next day. As she snuggled down, Annie thought she saw two shadowy figures moving silently through the stone trees in the distance, she blinked and they were gone. 'I'm imagining things,' she thought.

Soon she and her son were in an uneasy asleep. While Violet, who'd snuggled into the hairy neck of Furgal for warmth couldn't settle at all. So, she abandoned the idea of sleep, flew to the nearest tree and perched on a branch that overlooked the clearing. It was lucky that she did. Moments later, there was a flash of light and two small bangs. Looking down she saw Annie and Tiblou in repose, grey and motionless. Violet realized with a jolt of horror they had been turned to stone. Although Furgal had not.

The fairy flew frantically round and round the clearing, trying to find out what had happened. Then she widened her search to the surrounding stone trees, but there was no clue there either. Had they fallen foul of some kind of curse peculiar to this forest or had some malevolent force attacked them with a spell? Violet didn't know, but it was clear that they needed help, so she flew down to the petrified figures that looked like something from the top of an ancient tomb and placed a hand on Tiblou's cheek. She realized immediately the only way to save Annie and Tibs was to try and reverse the spell. But how?

Recalling every fairy spell she had ever cast, Violet tried to release her two companions but it was all in vain. Eventually, she gave up and dropped down to sit on Annie's stone hip where she sobbed until she felt sick. What should she do now? She toyed with the idea of going to fetch Chet, but it was a long way back from here. Besides, she was not sure she'd be able to find him easily and, more importantly, what could he do anyway? The stone figures of Annie and Tibs had obviously been created by a black spell. Chet was not a wizard like his brother; he only had brute strength. And no amount of hammering and chipping would release the stone prisoners. In fact, it could seriously hurt them. They were not inside some kind of shell; they were now made of stone through and through. So, if by some miracle this spell was reversed sometime in the future, they didn't want to come back to life with a hand missing or large chunks hacked out of one of their legs!

Violet sat there for a very long time not knowing what to do. Then, for some reason she couldn't fathom, she felt a strange sort of calm come over her and she knew something special was about to happen. There was a buzzing in the air, a magical vibe, that radiated goodness in this cold, hard place. Looking up, she saw the figure of Balgaire – her beloved Balgaire – hovering quietly in front of her.

'Oh, you've returned to us!' she cried, flying up to embrace him. But the vision of the wizard held out one arm to stop her.

'Only in spirit,' Balgaire's whispery voice sounded other-worldly. 'I can only return when forces of evil threaten this ancient woodland and its inhabitants, and, only until Tiblou gains his majority. As my successor, it is written that this is not his allotted time to die.' Then the flickering vision reached out a gnarled finger and touched Violet's fairy wand with one finger.

'Now try again,' whispered Balgaire. 'You should find...'

His sentence remained unfinished. Pleading for her lifelong friend and mentor to come back and never leave her again, Violet watched the pale figure fading out of view. Her sorrow was soon replaced by a fierce determination to take advantage of the late wizard's ghostly reappearance. Gripping her wand tightly in her tiny fist, she flew down and hovered half-way between Annie and Tibs.

'*SOLVE PETRIUM,*' she chanted, the words coming into her mind completely unbidden. '*SOLVE PETRIUM, SOLVE PETRIUM.*' She yelled hitting each one on the back.

There was another flash of light, two more bangs and muffled cries of fury in the distance. The stone figures began to fade in and out of focus like pictures on a faulty computer screen. The stone turned to liquid sand and fell away like slime disappearing into the ground revealing two skeletons, still curled in foetal position. Believing that she had overdone the Solve Petriums, a horrified Violet watched as the bones began to fuse together and translucent flesh gradually cover them until they were recognizable as Tiblou and his mother. Within a few minutes they tried to rise unsteadily to their feet. Annie sat down hard, holding her head and groaning. Tiblou dashed to the nearest stone tree and was sick. Annie pulled a water bottle from her bag, took a swig and offered the rest to Tibs.

'What happened?' he asked.

'It's a long story,' answered Violet. 'I'll fill you in as we go. But we can't stay here a moment longer. It's not safe.'

'But we can't walk through the forest at night...' began Annie.

'Yes we can,' argued Violet, starting to glow with a bright purple light. 'Follow me, please. There's somebody or something lurking in this forest that wants us all dead. Let's not give them another opportunity.'

So, with Annie mounted on Furgal again and Tibs walking unsteadily beside her, the sleep starved travellers set off through the second half of the Stone Forest with the pulsating mauve figure of Violet weaving about in front of them like a giant firefly.

CHAPTER EIGHTEEN

NIP THE KNOCKER

When he reached the bottom of the mighty stone staircase that led to the underworld, Aron was already beginning to have doubts that he was doing the right thing. Having run so far and so fast to escape the Swoopers, the back of his legs ached ten times worse than his sister's had done as he stepped off the final stair and looked around the great cavern at the bottom. Unlike Larna, however, he had never visited Lower Sherwood before, so this was a new and terrifying experience. Added to that, he did not know where to go. She had been looking for the lake where she hoped to find Cai; he was just looking for her and hadn't got a clue where to begin. After a couple of steps something crunched underfoot and he saw a flicker of light. Picking it up he groaned loudly when he realized it was Larna's mobile phone, smashed to smithereens. At least he had proof that his sister had been in the cave. He was getting more accustomed to the dark and anxious to get a move on but couldn't decide which of the tunnels to make for, so chose the nearest one and hoped for a miracle.

'This one gives me good vibes,' he said out loud, his voice sounding distorted in the echoing underground cave. He knew perfectly well it didn't – the tunnels all looked and felt exactly the same – but he had to believe in something to keep his spirits up.

It proved a terrible choice. The tunnel was full of spiders. Not ordinary spiders like the ones he had seen scuttling across the bathroom floor or sitting in the middle of a delicate web in the attic. Aron wasn't bothered by them. But these were big brutes with red eyes and huge legs that had threatening looking hairs sticking out all over them, like the tarantula his friend Dan Hall kept in a tank in his bedroom and allowed to walk up his arms. Aron was scared of these monsters and hurried past each one he encountered, watching it warily to make sure it didn't move or attempt to attack him. Fortunately, the spiders seemed to want a quiet life just as much as he did and none of them did anything more than glare resentfully at the disturbance he was causing in their tunnel. At one point he turned a corner and ran straight into a huge web that was strung across between the walls.

The fibres were sticky and clung to his face, making him scream in disgust as he clawed them off with his hands. He saw a rogue spider respond to the vibration. Descending like a paratrooper on a single rope to do battle it spat out a thread at a terrified Aron; he ran like mad, pulling at strands of gluey web stuck across his face and mouth.

As he ran he felt the walls with the flat of one hand. The stones glowed for a few seconds, long enough for him to see a few feet in front of him until the tunnel widened out and the spider disappeared.

At first he made good progress. The ground was firm beneath its covering of Turquoise sand and he was able to stride forwards with speed and confidence. But suddenly the earth gave way and Aron found himself floundering as if in deep water. He struggled on, wondering desperately what he was going to do now, until his feet struck solid ground under the surface. Brushing the sand aside with his hand he revealed a path running just below the surface.

'Saved!' he shouted as his voice echoed. Gingerly, he tiptoed onto the spot he had cleared and then put his foot forward to test where the buried path continued ahead of him. Then another tentative step...then another. In this slow, methodical way, he inched his way forward step by weary step, constantly fearing the path would run out and he would sink again. On a couple of occasions, he fell off the path, but was soon able to locate it again and, scrambling back onto it gratefully. He continued carefully on his way until he came to an area of white rocks and knee high piles of stones which looked like an abandoned graveyard.

Suddenly feeling exhausted, he lay down and curled up into a ball like a frightened animal.

And that's where he was found by a group of ghostly figures.

* * *

Had he known how close Larna was to him physically, Aron's despair may not have been so great. But, given their two equally desperate situations, they were actually as far apart as the earth is from the moon. Larna was back in the tiny courtyard, chopping logs again after a short night's sleep. The Boggret guards had woken Killian's slaves long before dawn, dispatching Zeb and June to their daily tasks in the castle kitchen preparing all sorts of food that nobody in the underworld ever ate, except Killian. Meanwhile, Larna was given a slightly bigger axe and told she must work twice as fast.

About mid-morning, Larna's hands were throbbing, in spite of wrapping them in her socks so they wouldn't blister. As she carried the heavy load inside, sweat ran down her tired face in salty rivulets that stung her eyes. She stopped to wipe her face on the back of her hand when Killian appeared and grabbed her roughly by the hair.

'I have another job for you,' he snarled, dragging her towards the door. The Boggret guards seemed extra-wary of their master today as they nervously, pushed and prodded her towards an area where there were many knee high piles of stones.

Warning bells rang in her head...she thought, 'Oh my God, this is their cemetery.'

Killian handed her an unusual implement. 'Dig me a trench,' he commanded, 'Three bodies deep.'

'What?' gasped Larna, her eyes wide with alarm. Seeing the king glower at her furiously and raise a club in his right hand to strike her, she cowered, hands up to protect her head. Shaking with fear she cried, 'I c-can't, I'm not s-strong enough...even if I could it would t-take me forever.'

'Yes you can!' roared the King, his face contorted with fury. 'You will work at it as if your life depends on it. In fact, your life **does** depend on it. If I'm not satisfied with your progress, I will kill you slowly and painfully and, my tribe will make your new friends watch your demise. They would enjoy that. They are a bloodthirsty bunch.'

Larna began digging straight away, her pathetic spade making almost no impression on the hard-packed ground. Her spirits sank to their lowest ebb. She wept as she worked, cursing the day she'd been stupid enough to follow her heart and get herself into this terrible predicament. If only she had stayed with the others and not wandered off alone. If only she hadn't brought that wretched wand back and then hidden it without telling her gran. If only she was enjoying a peaceful and relaxing summer holiday like the rest of her friends. But all these 'if onlys' were futile. She had no choice but to endure It. The alternative was too frightening to contemplate.

By mid-morning she was allowed to return to her cell for a short break. She crawled into a corner, absolutely shattered. Zeb and June were already in there, Zeb nursing a painful black eye inflicted on him by the king. They looked particularly frazzled and ponged to high heaven.

'He's in a foul mood today,' commented June, dabbing Zeb's swollen eye with a little of their paltry water-ration.

'Word around the camp is...' said Zeb, but his sister told him to save his strength.

'I'll tell Larna,' she said. 'You rest.' She dabbed a bit more and then turned to their young companion. 'Killian received some bad news today.'

'Good!' exclaimed Larna.

'Not good, he takes it out on us...' commented Zeb and received an exasperated sigh from June. 'He's had us cleaning out their stinking latrines.'

'And I'm digging a hole in the cemetery three bodies deep.' Larna quickly cut in.

After a shocked silence, a resigned June said, 'I try to listen when our tormenters grumble. It seems Killian had a couple of nephews who escaped from Tophet, this Boggret hell, years ago, when he murdered their father and took control.

'You told us you've already had dealings with one of the nephews, the black wizard Mordrog's apprentice, Edsel, who pushed his master into a vortex to inherit his wand; Thankfully, you said Tiblou rendered him harmless by turning him into a rat. But, what you don't know, Larna, Edsel had a younger brother called Flint who also escaped during the massacre and is currently planning a bloody coup, overthrow his uncle and reclaim what he believes is rightfully his. The Banjax family seat of power. Apparently he's in hiding somewhere in Upper Sherwood.

'Killian sent up a hit-squad of Boggrets to eliminate his nephew, but they failed catastrophically. I heard that what was left of them returned bloody and beaten saying Flint had given them the slip and was still at large. I shudder to think what fate he's planning for those Boggrets. The King has a murderous temper and doesn't tolerate failure, by anyone.'

'So that's why our lord and master is being even more cruel than usual today,' concluded Zebedia.

Larna had lots to think about as she continued her backbreaking dig. But the threat that Killian's younger nephew posed to the kingdom seemed of little interest to her personally. If he were to invade the underworld and depose his uncle, she had no doubt everyone would remain his slaves and she would just exchange one tyrant master for another. No, what was bothering her were the visions of Cai that she had experienced. She'd had another one last night as she slept fitfully for a few precious hours. So the visions weren't anything to do with the evil king. It really *was* Cai she was seeing. That meant he was alive and maybe close by. The thought of that gave Larna renewed hope and strength to continue her work. But they were only visions. When the excitement of what might be was replaced by what really was, Larna knew she was wishing for shadows.

CHAPTER NINETEEN

FIRE AND FLOOD

The rocky plain between the Forest of Stone and the Valley of Ice was dreary in the extreme. There was nothing to see in any direction other than brown rocks of various shapes and sizes. The path they were following led between them, zig-zagging left and right around the boulders and occasionally being blocked by a landfall. These were the most difficult obstacles to overcome, everyone finding it hard work to scramble up one side of the stony blockage and back down the other – especially shaggy mule. When Annie ran out of apples and had to rely on lots of encouragement to keep the animal going, he stayed loyal and continued to carry his rider along the winding path. When they reached a final landfall, with the Ice Valley clearly visible in the distance, they stopped for a breather and Annie dismounted. Realising that no more apples were forthcoming, the creature turned tail and lumbered back the way they had come like a grey shadow disappearing into the mist.

'Come on,' said Violet, 'It's only right, the mule should return to where it belongs.'

'I'm not sure I can continue,' Annie moaned.

'Yes you can' said Violet. 'We're nearly there.'

But Annie looked up, an expression of anguish on her face. 'It's not the physical effort,' she murmured. 'It's all the stress. I can't cope with it like you can.'

They took a short break to give Annie time to recover. As they sat there, Tiblou realized how much worry and danger they had come through already. No wonder his mother felt exhausted. When he thought back, their lives had changed dramatically since Balgaire's death. He still felt the loss off his friend.

Shaking his head as if to clear away all the dreadful trials they had endured so far, Tibs helped his mum to her feet and down the rocky path.

* * *

As they drew slowly nearer to Edina's heartland, the air grew noticeably colder. An icy wind blew in gusts across the terrain and patches of frost and ice could now be seen on the cold and lifeless ground. Annie had packed jackets, lightweight ones rolled up tightly into a tiny bag. Taking one out, she put it on and zipped it up snugly to her chin.

'I'm afraid I didn't have one small enough for you,' she told Violet.

'I don't need one, thanks,' replied Violet, shaking her head proudly. 'I can keep warm by flying about all the time.'

But Annie doubted the truth of the fairy's words. She looked cold and, from time to time, gave a shiver from head to toe that made the light from her wings shimmer like cold, blue moondust.

Luckily, there were trees at the start of the valley and Tibs was able to gather wood for a midday fire. Annie still had some packets of dried soup in her bag and they could boil this up with some melted snow from a small drift beside them. But the wood was frozen and damp, refusing to light when the young wizard put a match to it.

'Here, I'll do it,' called Violet, nudging him holding her tiny wand aloft. Normally able to magic up a small fire, the fairy failed on this occasion, despite repeated attempts. She swooped away, angry and defeated, to sit on a nearby branch. The others left her alone, knowing her brittle pride was hurt by failure and she needed time on her own to recover.

'Since Edina didn't suddenly appear after your last spell, do you think you could manage to light a fire for me Tibs?' urged Annie, holding out her concertina can pile up with snow. 'We're all hungry and need something warm to eat as soon as possible.'

So, reaching hastily inside his coat, Tiblou took out a wand and cast a spell at the pile of sticks on the ground in front of him. No fire sprang up. 'That's strange,' he murmured, casting the spell again. Still nothing happened.

'Are you okay?' asked Annie, anxiously. 'Have you completely lost your powers?'

'Of course not, mum,' snapped Tibs, trying not to sound as irritable as she had earlier. 'I'm fine.'

'Then why won't the fire start?' asked Violet, flying down from her perch with a frown of consternation on her tiny face.

'Oh, damn it, I didn't realize it would lose this amount of power.' said Tibs, shaking his head miserably. The young wizard decided to have one last try.

'I'll use a different spell,' he told them, 'hopefully a more powerful one, fingers crossed. Normally I wouldn't dream of using this, but as the wood refuses to light I reckon it needs something with a kick to get it going.'

He raised the wand. **'COMBUSTIUS INCENDO!'** he chanted.

'No, *Stop!*' shouted Violet.

'Why, dear?' asked Annie crossly. 'The flames are starting to come up quite nicely...'

'What the blue blazers...?' A look of bewilderment turned to shock when Tiblou took a closer look at the wand in his hand.

'You're using the *wrong one!*' yelled Violet. 'That's the fake we're giving to Edina. No wonder it doesn't work properly – it's not primed with genuine magic. That spell will go out of control.'

One look at the flames starting to spread across the ground towards them convinced Tiblou she was right. Pushing the wand back inside his coat and pulling out the right one, he tried to quell the flames with another dousing spell. It only worked in places, quenching the roaring flames with a hiss, but these patches of calm were soon overcome and the blaze continued on its way like a live animal.

'Run!' screamed Annie.

Although another shock like this was the last thing she wanted, she led the way as they fled from the flames, adrenaline firing her up to renewed efforts of endurance and survival. Tibs remained close on her heels, carrying Violet on his shoulder in case one of the many blazing sparks shooting into the air caught her gossamer wings and set them alight.

The fire seemed alive, snaking after them down the icy path into the Valley of Ice like a pursuing beast.

'How much longer before the spell runs down?' Annie shouted, looking over her shoulder with her breath coming in painful gasps.

'I don't know,' Tibs gasped, 'I *really* don't know!'

Just when the fire was snapping at their heels like a persistent, angry dog, it faded away and the trio stopped and stood gasping for breath in the icy air.

'I thought we'd had it then...' puffed Tibs.

'It's not over yet!' squealed Violet, flying upwards to get a better view of what was heading towards them. A wall of water! Another sheet of the fire had slithered away in the opposite direction and engulfed a bank of snow. This had melted instantly and was now gushing down a slope on the side of the path like a tidal wave.

'Run!' Annie yelled again.

'No time!' replied Tibs. 'Hold onto a tree and stand firm. Otherwise we'll be swept away.'

With Violet hovering anxiously above the deluge, Annie and her son braced themselves as the freezing water engulfed them. It took their breath away, making Annie cough and gasp, and left them both soaked to the skin and shivering uncontrollably. The water passed on down the path where it drained away, the residue freezing into big crystals that lined the sides like sparkling lights.

'It's okay, mum, I can dry us both like I did before...'

But Annie wasn't listening. She started laughing, shaking uncontrollably with mirth at the absurdity of their situation. The other two knew it was partially hysterics, but it seemed a kind of release and was very infections. Before long, Tiblou and Violet were laughing as well, standing with tears running down their faces and aching sides.

'What are we laughing at?' spluttered Tibs.

'I have no idea,' howled Annie, breaking out into a renewed fit of giggles that made her whole body shake and water drip off her clothes.

* * *

Not far away, in her ice empire, Edina watched the scene playing out in her head, a smile of delight curled her lips. She had just tuned in and had not seen the use of the wrong wand, only its effects.

She looked across at her rival who'd been brought in from the tree to which she'd been frozen and stood in the corner like an ice-embalmed Egyptian mummy. Only her eyes were visible and they gazed out at her opposite number with a mixture of hatred and pleading.

Just then, Rufus and Refina burst in, chasing each other as usual. Rufus had found a dead squirrel, it's body stiff and decomposing, and was trying to shove it down his sister's neck. She had previously thrown it at him, hitting him in the face, and he wanted his revenge.

'Quiet!' bellowed Edina, massaging the sides of her head to indicate she was visualising. 'How can I possibly do my work with you two around.'

'Sorry.' They chorused insincerely.

'With respect, Mistress,' said Selka, emerging from his hideout in the ice castle where he'd been regurgitating the fish he'd eaten last night to enjoy the taste again. 'Maybe you'd like me to go and keep watch for the visitors. I'm a much more reliable person to do the job than these two spurtleberks.'

'The visitors are already here. We saw them over by the frozen pond.' Smirked Refina.

'What are you talking about?' snorted Edina. 'They're not here yet. They're playing with fire over by the pass.'

'No, they're not. We saw two...' began Rufus.

'Don't argue!' screamed Edina, pushing the scowling twins out of the castle. 'I know what I saw and what I saw was correct. Now get out of here!'

CHAPTER TWENTY

NIP THE KNOCKER AND THE LOXLEY SKIMMERS

Aron woke up suddenly. Sensing he was no longer alone, dread flooded through him in waves. He expected to look up and see the Boggrets. Larna had told him all about them during their rare discussions about their past experiences. They had terrified her with their ugly faces and guttural voices. Aron breathed in, thinking he would experience their ghastly smell his sister had described in such revolting detail, but it didn't come. Wanting to know who was with him and at the same time desperately not wanting to know, the terrified teenager continued to lay still. Then a thought hit him like an express train. If he was surrounded by Boggrets, they would not be waiting for him to make a move. They would have kicked him awake or turned him over with their feet to see he was dead. So whoever was there was not threatening.

Aron rolled over and found himself looking at the end of a long thin nose. Above that were two large amber eyes in a broad friendly face. He wasn't very tall, in fact when Aron stood up, he only came up to his waist. The man's hands were exceptionally large for his size.

'My name is Nip and I'm a Knocker. I have received a whisper message, via the Lumins, from Cai, your sister's friend, asking me to take you to him.' Said the stranger in a high pitched voice.

'I appreciate the offer of help, but where is Cai?'

'Waiting for us at the northern compound planning a rescue mission for your sister. So follow me.' Nip led the way down a winding white path between the tomb-like rocks until they reached a pool. The water looked warm, hissing and frothing like a bubble bath.

'I'm not getting in there,' cried Aron.

'Have to if you wish to see the prince.' Explained the Knocker, 'I don't like it any more than you, but, it's the safest way.' He put his huge hands together and motioned a dive.

'How can I breathe underwater?' asked Aron.

Nip shrugged his bony shoulders and replied, 'Same as me.' And handed Aron a mask. It was similar to the one Larna had worn when she'd escaped from the Boggrets with Cai fifteen months earlier. Except these had a Lumins light attached to the forehead instead of on a belt.

He pulled the balaclava-like contraption over his head and followed his new friend towards the bubbling pool. He invited Aron to follow and found, as he dived into the depths, that he was able to breathe as easily as he could on dry land.

The pool, like the distant lake which Larna had headed for and visited in vain, was another entrance to a deep underground sea of crystal clear water beneath the rocky surface of the underworld. This was the Undines' domain. They were safe here from persecution by the Boggrets who naturally hated water and kept well clear of it. Despite the strangeness of the experience and his anxiety about finding his sister, Aron found himself enjoying the swim and marvelling at the mysterious underwater world and the many colourful fish that swam past him in all directions. He was almost disappointed when Nip indicated he should swim upwards and they broke the surface on a tiny beach. They had reached Cai's base which was above the level of the water. It stood on a small island and Aron went to take his mask off, but Nip stopped him.

'Leave it on for another few minutes, it will dry your clothes.' He chuckled, 'And mine too.'

The odd mix and match clothes worn by his companion was steaming as they walked towards the base and, when he looked down, Aron saw his own clothes were doing the same. By the time they reached the plain front door of the abode, he was completely dry. So he handed his mask back with a grateful smile.

Expecting a servant to open the door, Aron was surprised to see Cai himself waiting to welcome him. 'You came.'

'How did you know I was down here?' his old suspicion starting to return.

Cai explained, 'Our friends the Lumins watch you since you arrive underground. They watch everything, and report. Come inside. Much to discuss.'

As Aron entered, Nip bid them farewell, his job was done. Aron and Cai thanked him profusely for his help. Cai led Aron into a modest room with light green walls and offered him a seat on a plain wooden chair.

Cai sat across from Aron and, for a few seconds looked at him steadily. Then, to Aron's utter amazement, he leaned forward and buried his head in his hands.

Feeling emotionally uncomfortable, Aron asked, 'Are you okay?'

Getting up and pacing the room, his bare feet slapping on the floor.

'No, feel it my fault Larna here and **stinking Boggrets** capture her.' Angrily, he thumped the top of his chair.

'The Boggrets have my sister?' Echoed Aron.

Cai nodded, 'Yes! Now, we rescue her.'

'How are we going to achieve that?' he begged.

Cai nodded to the chairs and they both sat down again. Then, in his strange broken English, Cai explained how he had recently stretched out to Larna in a dream scape. A terrible mistake because it had encouraged her to come looking for him. He felt he was to blame for the situation she was now in. Hence his show of emotion. He explained that the Lumins, the living dots of light on the caves ceilings, had seen Larna appear in the underworld and, whisper messaged him that she'd been captured by the Boggrets. Some of the Lumins had followed them and reported that Killian was subjecting Larna to unspeakable cruelty. Also, two hairy creatures, who'd been there for years, had befriended her.

Aron's face blanched. 'Oh God, Cai, we've **got** to get her out of there.'

'Yes. Before it too late.' He went to one of the walls and pulled open a door. Aron followed him through and saw row upon row of short bows. Beside them hung quivers containing the arrows.

Aron frowned, mystified. 'What are *they* doing here?'

'Loxley Skimmers here for protection against Boggrets, and rescue Larna.' Stepping to the nearest arrows Aron raised his hand. 'Don't touch...tips poisonous, knock you out.' Cai warned.

Pulling back Aron was about to query 'Loxley?' then thought better of it.

Exiting the weapons room, they were met by an Undine of unusually large proportions. It was obvious that Cai regarded him as a trusted friend by the way they twittered together in their peculiar water language. Coming to an agreement, they turned to Aron.

Cai solemnly said, 'We have plan...Ranok,' indicating his friend, '...we make two groups, better chance. You with Ranok.

'Brilliant!' exclaimed Aron, 'What are we waiting for.'

CHAPTER TWENTY ONE

BATTLE FOR FREEDOM

As the long back-breaking afternoon wore on, Larna had the feeling she was being watched. She'd had the same feeling many times before in the past. Back in Upper Sherwood and often at home (oh, how she ached to be in either of those places again!) she had sensed there were people shadowing her and following her every move. But she'd eventually accepted that as the norm. Never the less, it was unnerving. She was an ally of Neve and Tiblou, someone on the side of right and good, so it was only to be expected that the forces of evil would spy on her for one reason or another as the war being raged between them went on. But this was back-to-front. The forces of evil were all around her. So who could be watching her down here...and why?

Larna's thoughts were rudely interrupted by the unexpected arrival of King Killian.

'I've come to see how the work's progressing,' he said, sounding reasonable enough. Then he stood and looked at the shallow hole she had managed to dig in the short time she'd been given and his face went puce with rage. He thrust his arms straight down by his side and stamped one foot on the ground like a toddler having a temper-tantrum.

'Is this *All?*' he bellowed, the force of his anger making Larna shake uncontrollably from head to foot.

'P-Please, my Lord,' she stammered. 'I have not been digging for long and the ground is very hard. And this spade you have given me is not very big...'

The King, marching across and said in a threatening manner. 'I commanded you to perform this task and you have disobeyed my orders.'

'I haven't,' protested Larna, feeling bolder because Killian was being an ass, and totally unreasonable. 'I've worked as hard as I could and done my very best.'

The King lapsed into one of his terrifying silences.

'Are you arguing with me?' he growled, his cruel eyes blazing like hot coals.

'No, your Majesty! I'm telling the truth.'

'Then the truth better be,' he snorted, turning on his heel and striding away, 'that you finish this ten times faster...or it will be your last. That pathetic little trench you've managed to dig can be *your* grave and I'll bury you in it with pleasure.' When he had gone Larna tried to resume her digging, but she felt totally drained of energy and collapsed to the ground in a faint. This was all too much for her. She couldn't go on.

Watching from behind a pile of rocks opposite Killian's dwelling, Aron could not bear to see his sister being so maltreated and Ranok had to put a restraining hand on his arm to prevent him charging out of their cover and attacking the king single-handed.

'Be patient, Aron,' Ranok urged. 'We rescue sister very soon.'

There were two Boggret guards watching Larna work. One of them marched over and jabbed her to her feet with his pointed stick. Then, indicating to his partner that was going to get them something to eat, he wandered off leaving the other one on his own to guard the prisoner.

This was the moment to strike. Barely able to contain his excitement, Aron watched as one of Cai's warriors stood up, fitted an arrow to his short bow and fired. Without a sound, the arrow flew over to one side and then curved round in an arc, striking the Boggret guard on his bare arm. The creature's eyes opened wide with shock and closed again seconds later as the poisoned tip took effect and he hit the floor, completely unconscious, with an almighty thud sending up a cloud of dust.

'Now!' whispered Ranok. The warriors and Aron silently crept out to rescue Larna.

Bending over the shallow hole, trying to loosen a big stone with the useless spade, the first Larna knew what was happening was when she felt a cold green hand being clamped firmly over her mouth to stop her from crying out. She wondered what new nightmare was unfolding until she saw Aron approach her. He motioned her to quietly follow him and, all resistance gone, she stumbled after her rescuers back to the cover of the rocks.

'What? How?' she began, but Ranok cut her short.

'No time explain,' he said firmly. 'Must leave immediately.'

'No. We *can't.*' cried Larna.

'*What?*' gasped Aron, unable to believe his ears.

'Have you come to rescue me?' asked Larna.

'Of course we have, muppet!' retorted her brother. 'What do

you think we're doing here? Playing hide-and-seek?'

'I'm not leaving without Zebediah and June,' she stated.

'They're *alive? Here? Where?* queried Aron.

Larna nodded. 'In the kitchen.'

'But that would mean entering the lion's den ...'

'I'm not leaving without them,' repeated Larna, stubbornly refusing to budge.

Seeing the jut of his sister's jaw, Aron knew she meant every word. 'It's not up to me,' he said, looking towards Ranok.

'Orders are only rescue Larna.' said the patrol commander.

'Then orders changed,' called a voice from behind them.

Spinning round, the rescue party saw Cai approaching with more Undine freedom-fighters. They were all carrying bows slung round their shoulders and quivers of skimmer arrows.

'Wanted to make sure you rescued safely, Larna,' he explained. 'So brought more warriors.'

At the sound of his voice Larna felt her heart melt and, without thinking what she was doing, she rushed to him for an embrace. But he only held her for the briefest of seconds.

'No time now,' he said, pushing her gently away. 'Must fight.'

* * *

The Undines were all in position ready to attack. Knowing the way, Larna led them into Killian's den with the archers using their Loxley Skimmers to eliminate every Boggret guard they met on the way. Larna felt weak in strength, but strong in spirit, and immensely proud to be working alongside Cai as an important and valued member of the team. Aron was also filled with excitement because he'd been given a spare bow and quiver of skimmers making him one of the squad.

Whooshing like passing cars, the special arrows magically curved round through the air one after the other, striking all the other Boggrets as they went in search of June and Zebedia. Soon a strange silence hung over the place and Killian came out of his quarters to find out what was going on. Cai was waiting for him. The Boggret ruler exclaimed *'You!'* as he caught sight of the Undine Prince and set about him with his cudgel. Cai parried the blows before a Skimmer nicked Killian's cheek. The sleeping draught did its work instantly and the all-powerful leader who dominated everyone in his domain with ruthless cruelty collapsed to the ground like a sack of potatoes.

'The kitchens?' Cai whispered urgently to Larna. 'Sleeping potion not long wear off. Must find your people and go!'

June and Zeb were at the sink, jointly washing a huge iron pot in which they had cooked a stew of vermin, complete with fur for their greedy master. They stood like statues, transfixed with surprise and fear, as the rescue party burst into the kitchen and waited holding their bows.

Aron gawked at the pair. He likened them to a couple of scruffy Chew Baccas from Star Wars and nearly laughed.

Larna stepped forward. 'Come with us now,' she urged passionately. 'These are the Undines, our friends. They've come to save us!'

Needing no second bidding, they dropped the pot on the stone floor with a deafening clang and rushed to the door, expressions of joy and disbelief on their faces.

'This feels like a dream,' whispered June.

'I agree,' said Larna. 'Let's hope we don't wake up back in the cells, eh?'

Some of the Boggret guards, those that had been struck first by the drug-tipped arrows, were just showing signs of stirring. All the Undine troops regrouped outside Killian's domain and set off together.

'Hurry, hurry,' cried Cai. 'May have time to get away. May not!'

Larna feared that Zeb and June, being older and worn out from years in captivity, would slow the party down, but it proved to be quite the opposite. Boosted by the possibility of freedom, like birds being released from a cage, they raced along with the rest of the group showing no signs of fatigue. Ranok and his troops were strung out either side of them. Larna and Cai took the lead while Aron and a young Undine brought up the rear.

'Where are we going?' yelled Larna.

'To staircase,' replied Cai. 'Must get you all to upper world immediately.'

'What about you?'

'Return to lake. Safe there.'

Both Larna and Aron remembered how far away the staircase was and how difficult both their journeys had been through the tunnels that led from the cavern at the bottom. They rounded a bend and found themselves on the banks of a fast-flowing stream.

'Wait!' ordered Ranok, holding up his hand.

The teenagers expected to be given masks and everyone told to plunge into the swirling water, but that was not the plan this time. At a command from Cai, a group of shimmering green turtles appeared from under the water and lined up along the bank like pedalos waiting to take holidaymakers for a boat ride on a lake.

'Are these...?' began Larna.

'Yes, living water-mounts,' said Cai. 'Get on now.'

Larna scrambled onto the hard flat shell of the leading turtle, holding each side to steady herself and gain her balance. Rapidly, the others did the same, with June and Zebedia in the middle of the flotilla, until they were all ready to go. Cai boarded his water-mount behind Larna and waved his arm forwards.

'Go!' he commanded.

It was an exhilarating ride, like something from a theme park. For a few moments, Larna and Aron forgot the desperate seriousness of their situation and focused on the thrilling ride, leaning first to one side and then the other as the current hurtled the turtles downstream like high-speed motorboats. They seemed to reach a tunnel leading to the stairs in a matter of minutes and, scrambling off, everyone stood shakily on the shoreline to steady their land legs before Cai led them through the tunnel, touching the walls to light their way. Aron's giant spiders were in the centre of their webs, watching their progress.

But, as they emerged into the cavern, their luck changed. In the semi darkness, they found their way blocked by a unit of Boggrets. They had not been sent by Killian. The enemy just happened to be there, one of the many raiding parties that regularly patrolled looking for plunder and slaughter. Their eyes lit up at the prospect of further victims standing in front of them like a line of startled rabbits.

* * *

Larna and Aron could not believe what was happening when, at a nod from Cai, Ranok held up his hand and signalled the archers to take up their positions round the cold, damp walls as if in surrender. The Boggret patrol was surprised, looking at each other with leers of delight on their grotesque greenish faces. They had just started to move forwards, sticks and axes poised to create a bloodbath, when they realized it was a ploy. Their gleeful looks changed to wide-eyed fear and then oblivion as, all together, the Undine fighters produced their bows from behind their backs and released the last of the Loxley

110

Skimmers into the air.

Facing Larna, 'You must go,' he said urgently, holding her at arm's length. 'Not safe here a moment longer.'

'Come with us, Cai,' she begged.

'Not possible, Larna,' he told her.

'Why not?' she cried, disappointed, panic in her voice.

'You know why not,' he replied, calmly. 'You human. Undines live in underworld. You upper world **and** another time. Not possible. Just not possible.'

Larna knew what Cai was saying was true. She remembered thinking the same thing over and over again as she'd lain in her bed unable to sleep or toiled at the exhausting tasks set for her by Killian. It had kept her going. But she didn't want to hear it put into words. It hurt too much.

With a bellow of blood-curdling fury, the King of the Boggrets burst out of the tunnel with more of his snarling troops. They all looked groggy, some scratching their open skimmer wounds, but it was clear they all had the same thing in mind – revenge.

Although the Skimmers returned to their owners, the drugged tips had all run out and the arrows would have little effect without them. So the Undines threw them aside and grabbed the discarded weapons of the Boggret patrol that lay on the ground beside their sleeping owners.

'Make a wall' ordered Ranok, using the time-honoured tactic to halt an advancing enemy. As his brave troops lined up, Cai leaned forward and gave Larna a farewell kiss before forcefully propelling her towards the steps.

'There is mate in your world,' he called. 'I see in mind's eye. He for you in time. You will know.' Then he turned to join the fight, leaving Larna to start her long climb to freedom behind Zeb and June.

Aron glanced back and saw one of the Undines fall after receiving a murderous blow to his skull from a shrieking Boggret with a fire lance and whirling spiked cudgel. He turned to rush back down the stairs again.

'*No!*' screamed Larna. 'You can't help him now. The Undines are sacrificing themselves so that we can escape.'

Reluctantly, realising the truth of her words, Aron headed on upwards. But, she couldn't resist looking back one last time and her heart lifted as she saw Cai and Ranok overcome a group of Boggret fighters and make their way down the tunnel towards their turtle boats and, having to leave the bodies of their fallen comrades behind.

Now was not the time for tears, though, and hoped against hope they would escape.

The climb to the top of the spiral staircase was twenty times worse than the descent. The front of Larna and Aron's legs now throbbed unbearably and they both wondered how Zeb and June were faring. But they seemed fired up by the prospect of freedom and they soldiered on, one step after another, gasping and panting but not complaining. Now Larna wished she had counted the steps because she had no idea how much further there was to climb. The staircase seemed to go on and on, up and up, with no sign of the cave at the top and that narrow crack leading to safety. She was beginning to think it couldn't be long now and they were going to make it when she heard a sound that filled her with dread. The others heard it too, stopping momentarily to look at each other in stricken horror. King Killian and the Boggrets were coming after them and didn't sound too far behind.

The stairs saved them. The people who built castles years ago in Robin Hood's time knew all about fighting. They knew that most people were right-handed, so that anyone attacking up the steps would be at a great disadvantage because the spiral shape prevented them from using their weapon arm.

Above them, however, the defenders had free use of their right arms and could strike downwards with power and ease. The four fugitives had no weapons but, they had their hands to hurl missiles, feet to land solid kicks. Time after time, the Boggrets scrambled up again looking increasingly battered and bruised, only to be sent tumbling down again in a heap. In the end, bellowing with fury, Killian decided to do the job himself and surged upwards to recapture his slaves. Larna took great delight in putting her foot in his face and sending him crashing downwards. He was bigger and heavier than all the other Boggrets – the result of all the meals he had devoured when everyone else went hungry – and his downwards motion gathered momentum as he crashed, head over heels, round every bend right to the bottom. Larna couldn't see if the fall had killed him, but she didn't care. He was gone. That was all that mattered.

With an unaccustomed silence filling the stairway again, they made it up the last few stone steps and staggered across towards the slither of light shining in from outside like a beacon.

CHAPTER TWENTY TWO

FIGURES IN THE MIST

Chet had spent an enormous amount of time searching in vain for Larna and Aron. As night began to fall again after a whole day of criss-crossing the open terrain, staring at the ground for any clue to their whereabouts, he felt tired and defeated. He returned to the campsite where they had been attacked by the Swoopers. The remains of the tents were still there, which he managed to make into the crudest of shelters by covering the frame with brushwood, and so he'd made this his base. There was also some dry wood and, after several attempts at rubbing two sticks together, as his father had taught him, managed to make enough sparks to light the wood. He fanned it until he had a small fire enabling him to heat a little of the dried food Annie had left him in the bottom of his rucksack. He decided to give up for the day and resume his search first thing the following morning.

With nourishment inside him, he felt a little better and settled down on the rough ground to try and get some sleep. Despite his aching weariness, he found it difficult and he wasn't sure whether he'd drifted off into a dream or not when he heard voices. They were more like an echo, very faint and in the far distance. Was this his brain telling him what he wanted to hear or was it real? He sat up with a start, his head hitting the brushwood roof of his makeshift shelter knocking it off. He crawled out and stood up, listened intently for a long time but heard nothing else. He must have imagined it. Yet something drew him towards the big clump of rocks some way away from the camp. He was sure the voices he had heard came from that direction. Unable to settle again, he set off to investigate. He remembered Annie's warning about not getting stuck in the crack, but he resolved to look through it again in case there was something inside. He very much doubted it. There was no reason to suppose anything had changed since he'd told his mother it was almost undoubtedly a dead-end. But there was no harm in checking it out and so he set off down the long path to the outcrop.

The up draught from the fissure smelled stale and damp. Chet sniffed, screwed up his nose then tried, and failed, to squeeze through the opening. Thoroughly disheartened he gave up, made his way down the hill and went in search of Larna and Aron. In the opposite direction.

* * *

Larna realized it was moonlight, not the sun, shining through the narrow gap they were aiming for.

Aron was utterly exhausted. He'd hardly slept the previous night in his desperate search for his sister. Since then he'd been into battle with the Boggrets and escaped with his life by a whisker. He felt completely drained and longed to sleep for hours and hours like he did at home on a Saturday morning. But he knew that was impossible.

'We have to find Tibs and the others.' he said urgently.'

'How do we do that?' cried Larna, who was aching to sleep herself after her ordeal below ground. 'We don't know where they are!'

'We know they were here before we both went AWOL...' began Aron.

'We can follow them,' cut in Zeb, pointing to his canine nose and sniffing the air, 'I'm still part wolf and expert at tracking. I can spot, and smell, anything that has gone past.'

'Right then, that's decided,' announced Larna, flopping down on the ground and leaning her back against the rock with a grateful sigh. 'We can rest here until daybreak and then follow their trail.'

'No, we're wasting time, Larna,' said Aron, grabbing her hand and pulling her up again. 'We have to leave right now.'

'But it's dark,' protested June.

Zebedia pointed up at the full moon that illuminated the landscape. 'Day or night, with my animal sense of smell I can follow a trail. Come on. Aron's right. We have no time to lose if we are to catch up with the others.'

Because Annie and Tibs had passed by earlier, Zeb was able to pick up their scent immediately. Suddenly excited, the four of them set off at a run, eager to catch up with their friends and family. Excitement and energy pumping through them once again, Larna and Aron forgot all about being tired and followed Zeb's confident directions towards the Stone Forest.

They were just disappearing into the rising mist when Chet arrived at the rock. Despite peering through the crack and seeing nothing, walking round it twice and spotting nothing, he could not shake off the feeling that he had missed something. But there was no evidence of it, so he trudged wearily back to his campsite to try to get a little sleep for the rest of the night.

* * *

Ahead of them, on the outskirts of the Valley of Ice, Tiblou and his two companions were also spending an uncomfortable and restless night. Annie was in a bad way. Her ankles were swollen and she found it painful to walk, slowing them down. There was still some way to go before they reached the bridge where they'd been told to meet Edina. He was worried she wouldn't make it. And time was running out. Fast.

'Not far to go now. Will you be able to make it?'

'Of course I will. I'm fine. Now go to sleep. We have a big day tomorrow.' Annie snapped.

But as dawn broke, Tibs could see Annie was anything but fine. She took a very long time pulling herself together and, as they prepared to depart, the look on her face made it clear she was in pain.

'Is she going to be all right?' whispered Violet anxiously, flying over and hovering beside his ear.

'I don't know,' he answered. 'She's losing the will to go on. She needs something to boost her flagging spirits and give her renewed hope, but I can't see where it's going to come from in this miserable, desolate place.'

Violet was the first to spot the bedraggled figures coming toward them out of the early morning mist. Like Elvan soldiers from a thousand years before Robin Hood's time, Larna and the others had half-walked, half-run throughout the night, with periodic rest stops through the Stone Forest.

'There's someone coming,' said the fairy in alarm. 'Quick. We must hide.'

Tibs grabbed Annie and they ran.

'Hello!' yelled a voice.

A distant memory made Annie stop dead in her tracks.

'If I didn't know any better I'd swear that sounded just like your dad.' She exclaimed. Turning round, she grabbed Tibs for support. Her eyes widened, mouth a silent O in utter astonishment.

'It's not possible.' cried Tibs.

Peering into the distance, Annie whooped, 'It is. **It. Is.** Look!' She shrieked, waving madly at the four figures appearing out of the mist like ghosts returning to the world.

'Tibs! Annie! Violet!' shouted Aron excitedly. 'It's us! We're back.'

'Look who we've found.' added Larna, excitedly.

Annie took one look at her husband and, her throbbing ankles completely forgotten, rushed into his arms and promptly burst into tears. They held each other tight for ages, the others watched in respectful silence tears running down their cheeks. Eventually the re-united couple parted and Annie embraced June while Tibs hugged his father.

'We never thought we'd see you again,' Tibs cried stepping back.

Zeb looked round and asked, 'Where is my eldest, Chet?'

'Chet remained behind with what's left of the tents in case Larna and Aron turned up.' Tibs explained. He beckoned Violet, 'Would you take him a message, to stay put. He'll be safer there and, a back-up if needed.

Violet nodded and flew off at high speed before Tiblou could thank her. Sighing with relief he moved over to be reunited with aunt June.

Annie turned to Larna and Aron. She hugged them both for a long time. Then she stood back and glared fiercely at them.

'Where have you been?' she scolded.

The teenagers simultaneously began to blurt out their stories, Larna keen to stress how her feelings had overtaken her and caused her to act so foolishly until Tiblou cut short her soul searching.

Breaking away from embracing his long-lost aunt, he swung his empty rucksack onto his back, checked that both the wands were safely inside his coat pocket and strode forward.

'I take it that you brought dad and aunty June up to date, Larna?' She nodded. 'So, come on, then,' he called. 'You can tell us everything that happened to you underground as we go along. We must get moving. If we don't make it to Edina's ice kingdom in time, everything we have gone through to find Neve will have been in vain. And that is not an option.'

As they set off in a long line to complete the vital last leg of their journey, Violet silently flew back and re-joined the group.

Annie took the lead, a smile of pure joy on her face and her discomfort forgotten. She held onto Zeb's hand the whole time.

'I'm never letting go of you again,' she told him.

CHAPTER TWENTY-THREE

WIND OF ILL FORTUNE

After only about half an hour of walking into the valley, with the early morning sun driving away the mist to reveal the chilling landscape of snow and ice-covered rocks, it became clear Aron was in trouble. He was virtually asleep on his feet, stumbling along like a drunken man and needing Larna to prevent him from collapsing in a heap. She wasn't in a much better condition herself. The adrenaline that had fuelled their search for the others and the euphoria they had experienced on finding them were now a thing of the past and the two teenagers felt drained. Utterly drained. Only willpower kept them going, but the need for sleep was becoming overpowering and could not be denied. Eventually, when her brother had to be prevented from sleep-walking into a wall of ice, Larna called a halt.

'We have to rest,' she called. Shivering, she buttoned her jacket and turned up the collar.

'You can't!' Annie told them, her usual motherly compassion overruled by the urgency of their mission.

'Yes they can, mum,' said Tibs, gently. 'We can afford an hour. No longer or we'll freeze to death.'

'That won't be enough!' protested Aron, flopping down onto a frozen rock, also feeling chilled. Holding his head in his hands he said, 'I could sleep for a week.'

'An hour will be enough, I promise you,' said Tiblou confidently. He went over and spoke to Violet. A few moments later they both nodded, obviously in agreement. With the fairy hovering behind him, the young wizard returned to their visitors holding Violet's tiny wand.

'Violet says, if I use this, I can grant you all one hour's sleep that will refresh you like a full night. I daren't use my own wand because I need to save what little power it may contain in case there is a dire emergency. Also, Violet has an idea that maybe, just maybe me using her wand may confuse Edina.'

'Suits me,' murmured the exhausted boy. 'This borrowed spell sounds like a great option. Let's go for it.'

Looking slightly comical, although nobody laughed, Tiblou

raised Violet's tiny wand and chanted, **'DORMUS BREVIAS!'** His breath chilled as he exhaled.

Immediately, the group curled up on the ground beside each other and slept soundly as if they'd been touched by one of Cai's Loxley Skimmers.

Exactly one hour later, they awoke and sat up, rubbing their eyes. As soon as they remembered where they were and what had happened, they jumped to their feet.

Stretching, Larna said, 'I feel great now!'

'Ready to go then?' asked Violet.

'You bet!' cried Aron, enthusiastically. He'd never felt so fit and full of energy in his life. 'That spell of yours was pure *magic!*'

Everyone laughed at this and Aron looked confused until he realized what he'd said. 'You know what I mean!' he added.

With the cold sun shining down on them from a clear blue sky, they headed on down the winding path that led to the bridge in the centre of the Ice Valley.

Everyone was in good spirits except Annie. She had something on her mind and hurried forwards to catch up with Tibs.

'I've been thinking, son,' she said, catching hold of his sleeve. 'Maybe you shouldn't carry the wand we're giving to Edina.'

'Why ever not?' he replied. 'It's perfectly safe inside my coat. I won't mix it up with my own wand again.'

'It's not that,' answered his mother. 'I just don't trust Edina. She will expect you to be the one carrying the wand and could well attack you to get her hands on it. Then she'd have what she wants as well as Neve. She'd have her cake and eat it, as they say.'

Tiblou thought for a moment and then nodded his head in agreement. 'Good thinking, mum,' he said. On the off chance that Edina was watching, he reached into his pocket and secretly handed the fake wand to Annie. 'Here you are, then. You carry it instead; I think it's a wise move.'

'See, I'm not just a pretty face,' said Annie, teeth chattering. She gave her son a loving hug and then dropped back behind him in the line, the all-important fake wand tucked carefully up her sleeve.

* * *

'Are you ready, my dear?' asked Edina, touching the ice-casing that imprisoned Neve with the tips of her fingers and causing it to fall to pieces with a series of shattering cracks. Rufus and Refina came rushing in to find out what was happening.

Oh, goody!' cried Refina excitedly. 'You're freeing the old bat. Can we torment her again now, please?'

'You don't know how to torment a worm,' scoffed her twin brother. 'Hand her over to me, mother. I'll make her turn our happy homestead into the Valley of Ice and Pain.'

'You'll do nothing of the sort!' snorted his mother, pushing him roughly aside to Refina's great delight. 'This *lovely lady* must remain quite unharmed from now on. She's very important to us. You all right, dear?' she mocked sarcastically.

Neve looked anything but all right. She stood in the cave, her shoulders drooping and her limbs shaking. Her eyes looked like two deep hollow sockets and her lips were blue and chapped.

'You won't get away with this...' she managed to whisper.

'Oh, but we can and we will,' retorted Edina, suddenly losing her false jollity and looking the malicious and deadly witch she really was. 'It will be all over soon and evil will triumph like it always should. You're just a pawn in the game, dear. So make sure you don't do anything stupid, otherwise your family will lose you as well as Mordrog's wand.' Leaning forward she whispered conspiratorially in Neve's ear, **'You** can go but **I'm** keeping your wand.' And with that, she gave the White Witch a shove and propelled her towards the entrance to the ice castle where Selka was waiting.

'Escort the prisoner to our hiding place overlooking the bridge and the crossroads,' she ordered him. 'When the time comes I shall freeze her to the tree again. Then we wait for our guests to arrive.'

'It will be a pleasure, Mistress,' replied the Kappa, bowing slightly to avoid the fluid contained in his concaved head from spilling onto the ground.

'Can we pelt her with stuff as she goes?' asked Rufus eagerly.

'No!' snapped his mother.

'Can we pelt Sulky then?' suggested Refina, clapping her hands together with glee at the prospect. 'It's a long time since we had some sport with him.'

'*No pelting*. That's childish.' ordered Edina, slowly and distinctly through clenched teeth. 'The moment I've been waiting for is about to come true. I'm not going to let you brats do anything to jeopardise it, do you understand?'

* * *

119

As the impressive castle and its bridge finally came into view, everyone gave a huge sigh of relief. But it was deserted.

'Where's Yaya?' asked Larna, expecting to see her grandmother waiting for them with her captors.

'I expect she's on her way right now,' Tibs told her. 'We've made the rendezvous with time to spare. Edina doesn't want to be standing around in the cold any longer than she has to…' He shivered. 'Although, with *her* cold heart she should be used to it.'

At a muttered command in the distance, which nobody was sure whether they'd heard or not, a whirlwind swirled out from between the rocks and headed straight for Tiblou. Everyone stood rooted to the spot with shock as it powered towards him.

Realising he was facing another attack, this one aimed at him alone, the wizard tried to escape the whooshing spiral but it pursued him like a hunting predator.

Annie screamed, 'Tiblou, watch out.'

Unfortunately for Tibs, Annie's warning came too late and the whirlwind engulfed him, sweeping him upwards into the air and suspending him upside down, shaking him like an old blanket. Everything fell out of his pockets and landed on the ground beneath him, including his wand. The whirlwind swept over this, picking it up and throwing it into the distance. Then it paused, as if waiting for a command, before returning to Tibs with treble its' previous fury and spinning him round and round until everyone watching felt giddy and sick. Then, like a dog being recalled by its master, the miniature tornado departed so that Tiblou hit the ground with a sickening thud and lay there groaning and holding his head. When he stood up, he lurched one way and then the other as he struggled to regain his balance. With his father's hairy arms supporting him, he managed to steady himself and stood nodding and swaying, his face the colour of chalk.

'Where's my wand?' he gasped.

'I'll get it,' cried Larna, hurrying away towards some distant rocks. She had kept her eye on it as Tiblou flew through the air and had noted where it landed. She returned with it a few moments later and handed it over.

'Thanks, Larna,' he said, a wan smile creasing his face. 'No damage done by the look of things.'

'It wasn't your wand they were after,' commented Annie. 'It's the one that's hidden up my sleeve.'

'Who's they, Annie?' asked Aron.

'Edina, of course,' she answered with a hint of impatience. 'Who else could it be? The cunning creature is trying to get her hands on the wand without letting go of Neve, just like I said she would.'

But, as she watched from her hiding place overlooking the bridge, waiting for the rendezvous, Edina's face was black with fury. That whirlwind was nothing to do with her. Someone else was here.

CHAPTER TWENTY-FOUR

THE EXCHANGE

The rendezvous had been set for during the hour of the blue moon, but the knowledge that there could be a threat to her well-laid plans caused Edina to panic. With a click of her fingers, she transported Neve from the hiding place above to the huge frozen tree by the bridge and imprisoned her against the trunk with ice that set like concrete down her back. Neve hung there like a string puppet, her arms and legs moving but her head held firm as if in a vice.

At that precise moment the sky darkened and the tableau was bathed in a silver-blue light from an unusually large rising moon.

Edina looked up, her skin was tinged with the cold blue rays emphasizing the jagged scar running down her face. 'You made it then. I know one old witch who's happy to see you,' she said, stepping aside.

Larna was the first to spot her grandmother. *'Yaya!'* she shouted, rushing over to be reunited with her grandmother.

'Don't touch the goods, girl,' warned Edina. 'Otherwise the same thing will happen to you.'

'Are you all right?' asked Larna, tears of joy and terror dripping down her cheeks.

'I've been better,' Neve answered with a wry smile.

The others hurried over and gathered round.

'Don't all talk at once,' croaked the old lady. 'I may be the guest of honour at this party but I'm not feeling very sociable at this moment.'

So everyone stood back. Aron went first, going up close to his grandmother to whisper, 'You'll be free soon, Yaya. We'll see to that.'

Then Tibs and Annie said similar words of reassurance before Violet flew over and hovered nearby, glowing a gorgeous purple light to show how pleased she was to see Neve again. The prisoner's eyes grew wide with surprise and delight as June and Zeb went up to her to say hello.

'Thought you were lost forever,' she whispered.

'No, we're back, thanks to Larna and Aron.' said Zeb with a

smile.

'*Enough!*' shouted Edina, clapping her hands like a fierce schoolmistress bringing her unruly class to heel. 'No more happy family reunions. Let's get down to business, shall we?'

Annie had quietly returned Mordrog's replica wand back to Tibs, he stepped forward and, without any ceremony, held it out to Edina. She rushed forward to grab it, her eyes alight with excitement like a greedy child in a sweet shop. But, at the last moment, he snatched the wand back and tucked it away inside his long coat.

'Not until you free Neve,' he said.

The witch stood rooted to the spot, seething with fury. 'What's the matter?' she snarled. 'Don't you trust me?'

'Not in a million years.' answered Tiblou. 'You're an evil witch bent on death and destruction. Why would I believe a word you say?'

'You insult me. I shall not return the White Witch to you,' she threatened petulantly.

'Then you won't receive your brother's wand,' countered Tibs, standing his ground.

A long silence followed. Stalemate. The black witch wouldn't budge, but neither would the young wizard. The others began to fidget with impatience and Neve's eyes watched everything with a mixture of fear and longing. Eventually, Edina gave in and nodded her head.

'Very well then,' she said, as if deciding she was only defeating herself by holding out any longer, 'I agree to release the prisoner.'

'Go on then,' called Aron, who was almost beside himself with the drama and tension.

'*Shhh!*' ordered Larna, crossly. 'Keep out of it, will you?'

Slowly and deliberately, Edina lifted her own wand and chanted, '*EXEAT OMNIUM!*'

Immediately, the ice binding Neve melted and she fell forwards from the tree, stumbling into the arms of Annie who ran to catch her.

'Are you okay?' she asked. 'You're *freezing*.' She removed her jacket and wrapped it round Neve's shoulders.'

'I am now,' she replied, teeth chattering.

Having completed her side of the bargain, Edina strutted up to Tiblou and held out her hand.

'Mine, I think!' she said.

The wizard nodded, reached inside his pocket and handed over the evil-looking black wand with great reluctance. Everyone held their breath. They knew he was acting, but didn't want to give the game away with any involuntary movement or facial expression on their part. And Tibs was acting extremely well. He looked downcast and defeated as if he'd just lost an all-important battle, and Edina was the winner. She certainly looked that way.

'**Yes**-s-s!' she whooped in triumph. 'My inheritance at last!'

With Larna and Aron supporting her on either side, Neve started to walk away with the others.

'Er, excuse me! Where do you think you're going?'

'Home,' answered Annie. 'It was a fare exchange, Edina. You have what you want, you hateful creature, and so do we thank goodness. Our business is done here. We don't need to stay a minute longer.'

'Always the insults,' complained Edina, brandishing her new wand in a menacing manner. 'I should be careful what you say from now on, old woman. Remember who has the power here now. And none of you are going anywhere before I demonstrate this power. I want to see what this beautiful wand will do before I allow you to leave.'

The witch put her fingers into her mouth and emitted a piercing whistle. Moments later Selka came slithering down the icy slope from the viewing place above like an obedient dog. Larna no longer needed to hold her nose as the Kappa passed. Having been a prisoner of the Boggrets, she was now used to revolting smells and Edina's pet odour no longer disgusted her. It was the same for Zeb and June. They just watched with a mixture of surprise and amusement as the Rufus and Refina.

'Stand back!' she commanded her children. 'This is the first time I've used my brother's wand and I know it has mighty powers. You might come to harm if you're in the way.'

With the twins waiting together at a respectful distance, the others held their breath again as Edina raised the wand to test it out. Would it work? Would she be convinced it had real magic powers? The moment of truth had arrived!

'Don't worry, Selka dear,' she said to her pet that was crouching on the ground in front of her. 'I'm just going to change you into something else for a moment. Don't worry. It won't hurt and I'll change you back again immediately. *Novo Kappa, Novo Kappa!*'

There was a thick puff of smoke and, as it cleared, everyone saw that Selka had been turned into an osprey. Instead of his unpleasant scale-like appearance, he was now a magnificent fish-eagle with whitish-grey feathers and a curved yellow beak.

'Why an osprey?' Larna whispered to Tibs.

'I could only empower the wand with good magic,' the wizard mouthed back. 'Selka's been changed from something ugly to something beautiful.'

Looking puzzled by the outcome of her spell but satisfied the wand was working, Edina raised it again to reverse the magic. But Selka had other ideas. Now was his chance! With a shriek of triumph, he spread his enormous wings and took off into the air. Then he circled round before nose-diving downwards and swooping low over Edina's head so that she had to throw herself face down on the ground. And the transformed creature wasn't finished yet. He turned on the twins to take his revenge for all the years of neglect and abuse they'd given him and, pooped droppings onto them. Then diving down time after time to peck at them until they were screaming for mercy. By now, their mother was back on her feet and holding the wand again. Catching sight of her out of the corner of his eagle eye, Selka broke off and swooped past her, knocking the wand out of her hand before she had a chance to use it.

He flew upwards, circled above Tiblou dipping his wings in thanks and farewell, and flew away into the distance, shrieking all the way with undoubted triumph at his unexpected escape into freedom.

'Don't think you'll see him again, Edina,' commented Violet.

'Shut up, you stupid little creature,' snarled the witch. 'Now get out of my sight, all of you.'

Tiblou and his friends didn't need telling twice.

'Come on, everyone,' he urged. 'We've both got what we wanted, so let's get the hell out of here. It's a long way home and we're all shattered, so the sooner we get going the better.'

'We'll soon have you back in Blithe Cottage having a nice cup of tea, Yaya,' chuckled Larna.

'I could do with it now,' sighed Neve. 'I'm **so** weak I couldn't even conjure up an escape from that mad woman.' She raked her fingers through her hair, thoroughly dejected. 'I'm no use to anyone at the moment.'

'Don't give up, where's your fighting spirit? Keep quiet and reserve your strength. You'll soon get your powers back, you'll see.' Larna said with utter conviction. 'Now, let's get going,' pointing to the long stony road leading back out of the valley towards the stone forest. But after a few steps they walked into a barrier they could not see. Aron, still suffering the vicious pecks from hungry Swoopers, fell to the ground bumping his nose adding to his pain.

'Ouch!' he yelled. 'What was that?'

'It's another invisible wall,' Larna informed him, just managing to prevent Neve from walking into it and injuring herself. The White Witch was still in a poor way, despite the boost of being free, and could not afford to sustain any more injuries.

Larna asked, 'Can you do anything, Tibs?'

The wizard ran up and felt the wall with his hands. It was solid. And it ran all the way round the castle, imprisoning everyone inside. Tiblou took out his wand to see if he could remove the blockage with one of his spells, but was immediately told not to bother.

'You won't be able to shift it,' said a scornful voice.

Next moment, a figure materialised in the centre of the bridge and a gasp of horror went up from everyone, including Edina.

'Hello, everyone,' mocked Edsel. 'Have you missed me?'

CHAPTER TWENTY-FIVE

SHOWDOWN

A long shocked silence followed the Boggret's sudden and totally unexpected reappearance.

Larna was the first to break it. 'We thought you'd been banished for good,' she said.

Aron grabbed her arm. 'No, sis! We hoped and prayed he was!'

'How kind of you to be so concerned about me,' mocked Edsel, looking the embodiment of evil with his cruel face and immaculate red warlock robe. 'You always were such charming humanoids. I shall miss you when you're gone.'

'Oh, don't start all that again,' scoffed Larna, looking at him in disgust. 'You don't scare us.' It was a complete lie, of course. She was completely terrified, her insides feeling like jelly, but had no intention of showing it.

Taking a lead from her granddaughter, Neve piped up. 'That's right, you were a little rat and you still are.'

'Oh, that's so witty, coming from the white witch who allowed herself to be kidnapped.' sneered the Boggret warlock. Then his face suddenly became furious. 'Yes, I was a rat. For a long time. And an extremely unpleasant experience it was too. But fortunately for me and unfortunately for you, your pathetic magic didn't last my lifetime. The spell that was cast over me wore off and, amazingly, I returned to myself.' He preened. 'And, as I was always very hungry, my first response was to eat all my fellow rats. *Alive.'* He licked his lips. 'Hmm. Delicious!'

Everyone made horrified faces at this and June leaned over feeling nauseous.

Tiblou stepped forward and confronted their old enemy. 'It was *you* who was responsible for all those mysterious attacks on us, wasn't it?' he said.

'Of course it was, dear boy,' mocked Edsel airily. 'Who else did you think it could be? Certainly not that ridiculous apology for a dark witch over there.' Nodding in Edina's direction.

Edina glared pure hatred at her rival and gripped her newly acquired wand even tighter as if he was going to snatch it out of her hand right there and then.

'So what were you hoping to achieve?' continued Tibs.

'What do you think?' snapped the Boggret, growing impatient. 'I wanted to get rid of all you goody goodies and have these dear people from the past Sherwood all to myself. Then they could tell me where they'd hidden Mordrog's wand. Alas, poor Mordrog, I knew him well. Such a sweet soul. I miss him **dead**~fully' He said, with a malicious grin at his play on words.

'So you ordered the coach attack...' Tibs spat out.

'Yes. **Yes!**' Edsel puffed with pride. 'The coach attack, the flesh eating flowers – they were a particularly delightful offensive, as well as the turning to stone ... and that other stuff. Pity it all failed, really, because I'd be rid of you already. But it doesn't matter now. Edina here has kindly done my work for me and the wand that I'm after is right here for the taking.' He snorted, 'And, the witch, Neve, has lost her power, so she's no use to you, or a threat to me.'

At that moment, a loud knocking echoed round the bridge, making everyone jump. They looked round and saw another Boggret, younger and not so handsomely dressed as Edsel, standing on the other side of the invisible wall.

'Let me in!' he mouthed, appearing to knock on thin air and making the urgent sound again. Edsel clicked his fingers and the barrier was removed, allowing the newcomer to stride up to the frozen tree and take his place beside the warlock. The Boggret body stench doubled immediately.

'Allow me to introduce my young brother, Flint. He, like me, escaped from Tophet, below, and our not so loving uncle, Killian. We are working to restore our rightful place as rulers of the underworld.'

'And this one too, in due course.' Flint looked round at everybody, his face a carbon copy of his brother's in its hatred and contempt for everyone surrounding him. He stopped when he caught sight of June and Zeb, looking surprised and curious.

'You!' he exclaimed, recognising them from his time underground. 'What are you doing here?'

The animal in Zebedia rushed to the fore, 'Hoping to rid our precious Sherwood from filthy Boggrets like you two and ugly witches like that old crone over there,' he snarled, all his hatred and resentment for the years of cruel captivity overcoming him for a moment.

Flint snorted, 'Such a pity your noble aims will all come to nothing. You and your hairy sister will soon be exchanging your new found freedom for captivity again, 'Enough of this chit-chat, brother!' Edsel cut in. 'We're wasting time here. Let's get about our business and be gone!'

The warlock looked round just in time to see Edina sneaking away with Rufus, Refina and the precious wand. They began to run, the witch streaking ahead of the twins in her desperation to escape with her prize. Edsel pointed his finger at them and one of the emergency spells he always kept in reserve zig-zagged from his fingertips in a flash of red fire. Edina and the twins were jerked backwards as if by an invisible rope and dumped on the ground at the Boggret's feet where they rolled around groaning. Larna and Aron were tempted to cheer at the ignominious fate of Neve's hateful kidnapper, but they both knew it was not the time and kept silent. This was getting serious. Two ultra-evil forces were now competing for possession of the fake wand and the consequences were bound to be overwhelming.

'Hand it over!' ordered Edsel.

'No!' retorted Edina.

'I said hand it over, you old crow!'

'And I said no, you thieving Boggret scum.'

This was too much for Edsel. He reached inside his robe and took out his own wand. He had fashioned this when he returned to being a warlock, imbuing it with the evil magic in his fingers and then using these spells to multiply its power. It was a fearsome weapon, though nothing like the awesome might of the genuine wand he sought to obtain. Edina did the same, pointing her witch's wand up at his face. Battle was about to commence.

'Let's go, Tibs,' whispered Annie, 'before the muck hits the fan.'

'I can't, mum,' he answered.

'Why not?' she insisted, her face looking even more determined than usual. 'We've rescued Neve, *those* two are about to take each other on and will be totally distracted for a while and they still haven't discovered they've been tricked. It's the perfect time to make our escape.'

'I just can't,' repeated Tiblou, his young face looking anxious and set at the same time. 'I have to stay and witness the outcome of this struggle. My future as a wizard and of both Sherwood's is at stake here. I *have* to know which one we'll be facing!'

Annie stamped her foot with frustration, but failed to argue further. She had total faith in her son's judgement, even though she didn't always agree with it.

In an attempt to deflect Edsel, whom she planned to lull into a false sense of security, Edina stepped forwards with a sickening smile on her face.

'We don't need to fight about this, my friend,' she cooed. 'Why don't we simply join forces, you, me and your brother? We could be a triumvirate, like they had in Rome back in ancient earth-time, the three of us ruling all of Sherwood together. Wouldn't that be something? I could command Upper Sherwood and you two...'

Edsel's response to her proposal was to loose off a spell that carried her backwards through the air, so she crashed against the petrified ice tree. She screamed as she hit it and slumped to the ground, senseless for a moment. But then she jumped up, her previous pleading manner replaced by raging hatred.

'**Nobody** does that to me!' she roared. 'Do you hear? Nobody! Then she held up the pseudo black wand. 'You forget I have this. And I shall use Mordrog's awesome power to annihilate you!'

Edsel's response was to issue another spell that knocked the wand right out of her hand and sent it slithering across the frozen ground. It came to a stop about half-way between them, lying there invitingly like a prize to be won. Edsel marched forward to claim it, but the moment he moved, his enemy released a spell of her own that lifted him right up into the air, turned him over and brought him crashing down head first onto the ground. Now it was Edsel's turn to be knocked out and, as he lay there motionless, Flint stepped forward to claim the wand in his brother's place. The same spell struck him, only this one left him hanging helplessly in the air for several minutes before he also crashed painfully back to earth. During the time he was suspended, Rufus and Refina begged to be able to pelt him with rocks, but their mother refused them angrily.

'Stay out of it' she shouted. 'Now is not the time for games. This is adult business.'

By now, Edsel had come to his senses and stood unsteadily on his feet, pointing his wand fairly and squarely at Edina. '**MORTUNA MORS VOBIS**' he chanted, sending a snake of pulsating light towards her. She screamed as it hit her, a ghastly other-worldly shriek that made everyone clap their hands over their ears with pain. They knew it was a death-blow.

Edina was about to lose the battle. The witch knew this too and had one final counter-blow in reserve. Writhing in agony as Edsel's spell was dissolving her away to nothing, she choked and coughed and finally brought something up into her mouth. It was a tiny dart coated with all the noxious poison from deep within her. With her dying breath, she spat the dart at Edsel's neck.

'**Mortuna Mors Vobis**; *die, ugly crone, die.*' And Edina the

Ice Witch was no more.

Grinning in triumph the Boggret warlock strode over and picked up the fallen fake wand. Edina's personal wand having perished with her.

'Mordrog's power is mine at last,' he proclaimed, holding it aloft. 'Now I shall become lord of Upper Sherwood!'

The twins were the first to realize the significance of this and, panicked.

'What happens to us?' cried Rufus.

'Shut up, you stupid fool!' hissed Refina, but it was too late. Edsel turned towards them.

Rubbing his neck where Edina's dart had entered, he snarled, 'Did you think I'd forgotten about you,' he raised his wand. 'We can't have Edina's poor motherless brats hanging around causing trouble, can we now? So I'll send you where you deserve to be.'

'Where's th-that?' asked Refina, looking suspicious and fearful. All the bravado she and her brother had shown in the past had evaporated now they were facing the same sort of heartless cruelty themselves.

'You're going to the kingdom of Tophet in the underworld,' announced Edsel. 'My *dear* uncle Killian has lost his three human slaves and desperately needs replacements, especially ones young and fit whom he can work to exhaustion.'

He yelled, *'EXPELLO TORA',* And the twins disappeared as well.

CHAPTER TWENTY-SIX

THE WHISPERED SECRET

Larna and Aron were standing either side of Neve with Tiblou and Annie. June and Zeb stood opposite, arms linked, with Violet hovering above them. The two groups looked at each other in terrified silence, June raising one eyebrow enquiringly and her look being met by an almost imperceptible shake of the head from Annie, warning her not to give anything away. But they all knew what was coming and only Tibs could save them now.

Edsel motioned to his brother. 'Come and stand behind me, Flint,' he called. 'I'd like you to witness this great moment at close-quarters and I wouldn't want you to be in the line of fire.' Then he raised the false black wand, pointing backwards and forwards between his enemies with obvious relish. 'I am a benevolent person,' he told them, 'so I shall make your mass execution quick and relatively painless. So goodbye to you all. It's been unspeakably tedious knowing you and I can't wait to see the back of you. *Mortuna Mors Vobis!'*

A flash of fire shot from the wand in his hand. But instead of dissolving everyone away, a circle of flowers grew all around them, their colourful heads waving and bobbing in the cold wind.

A dark frown appeared on Edsel's face, but he was prepared to give the wand the benefit of the doubt. After all, it looked and felt exactly like the wand he had lost fifteen months earlier and had no reason to suspect anything different.

Taking advantage of Edsel's confusion Neve pushed Aron and Larna behind her. Without her wand her power was greatly diminished.

'I imagine these are to mark your graves,' he said, 'or rather the spot on which you all disappeared from this world forever. So look around you for the final time, my friends. You won't see anything further except darkness.' And he cast the spell again. This time a stream bubbled up from underneath the ground, and began to flow round the circle of flowers. It looked strangely out of place in the barren landscape of the Ice Valley, but very beautiful and peaceful none the less.

Edsel didn't try a third time. Realising he had been fooled and the wand he was holding only contained the wrong sort of magic, he gave a bellow of fury that could be heard for miles around and snapped the fake wand in half over his knee.

'You **Fools!**' he seethed. 'Did you **really** think you could deceive me?'

'We didn't set out to deceive **you**,' Larna shouted back defiantly. 'We did it to trick Edina.'

'Shut up!' screamed the warlock, shaking both his fists at his side in a frenzy of rage. 'How **dare** you!' He stepped forward with the intention of hitting everyone in the face to give vent to his anger, but Tiblou barged forward and Edsel thought better of it. He became calm and calculating again.

'Flint,' he said softly. 'Grab those two Gorrys. By the wrists.'

Before anyone could stop him, the younger Boggret strode over, pushed Neve to the ground and grabbed Larna and Aron as instructed, twisting their arms painfully.

'*Aarg! Gerroff,* that hurts!' yelled Aron.

'Don't struggle,' shouted his sister, her own eyes watering with pain.

Flint dragged the helpless pair in front of his brother who strode round them menacingly.

'Now, tell me where the **real** wand is!' he demanded.

When the prisoners refused to answer, Flint gave their wrists another agonising yank.

'Tell me!' screamed Edsel, holding his wand.

Tiblou came to their rescue. Unable to witness this cruelty, despite the pair's undoubted bravery in the face of it, he stepped forward with his wand raised, praying that it held sufficient power.

'Leave them alone, Edsel,' he commanded, helping Neve to her feet. 'Let this be between you and me.'

'Well, then,' replied the Boggret, motioning to Flint to release his hold. 'I'll dispose of you first and then we can get back to business.'

Everyone realized the importance of the next few moments. This was the big one, the final battle between the forces of good and evil. Whoever emerged victorious would decide the future and what happened to all the different races and creatures that inhabited Upper and Lower Sherwood. It would be a fight to the death, a turning point in the forest's long and varied history. Larna crossed her fingers behind her back. So did Aron. They had witnessed wizard versus warlock battles before during their previous visit to the future, but this one seemed more important. Edsel and Tibs were fighting over the information stored in their heads concerning the real wand's hiding place. So they were the prize. It was a terrifying thought.

Feeling inadequate, Neve did what she could to protect her own and gently pulled her grandchildren behind her again.

Edsel and Tiblou took up positions opposite one another like boxers squaring up before the bell. The warlock, ever cunning and keen to catch his opponent off-guard, paused for a moment and looked up at the sky. Without thinking what he was doing, Tibs followed suit and a split-second later, seeing nothing there, he realized he'd been tricked. The next thing he knew, a thunderbolt flew from the end of Edsel's wand and exploding right in front of him with a bang that almost shattered everyone's eardrums. Tiblou was blown over backwards and turned several somersaults before coming to a stop in the frozen grass at the edge of the roadway. Edsel strode over for the kill, but the wizard just managed to roll aside in time as a knife shot from the end of his enemy's wand and buried itself in the ground where he had been a moment before.

Annie screamed and covered her eyes with her hands, momentarily distracting Edsel.

Now, Tibs had a chance to retaliate and test the strength of his wand. He released a counter-spell that engulfed Edsel in foul-smelling grey smoke that stung his eyes and made him stagger backwards, coughing and retching, green gunge dripped from his nose. Jumping to his feet, Tiblou realized it was his chance now to dispatch his enemy and raced over, but Edsel was waiting for him. Pointing his own wand directly into the wizard's face he screamed, *'Tey Blatteria!'* and Tibs instantly turned into a scurrying cockroach with Flint in pursuit trying to squash it. Jumping gleefully to his feet, he pointed the wand at Neve, Annie, Zeb, June and Violet in turn repeating *'Tey Blattaria!'* They turned into cockroaches too. Leaving them to scuttle together under a rock for safety, Edsel turned to Flint and indicated his brother should grab Larna and Aron again.

'Now, where were we?' he said.

The teenagers were now all alone with nobody to help them.

'You're wasting your time here,' shouted Aron, clenching his teeth against the pain in his arm. 'We don't know where Mordrog's wand is!'

'Don't lie to me!' shouted Edsel.

'It's true,' insisted Larna, trying to keep her voice calm to reason with the monster, even though she knew this was unlikely to do any good. 'Tiblou put a blocking spell on us.'

The Boggret obviously believed Larna because he told Flint to release them both.

'What sort of spell are we talking about here?'

'How the hell do we know?' retorted Aron, rubbing his throbbing arm and feeling bolshie. 'How do you expect us to know a thing like that, you idiot.'

'*Don't speak to me in that disrespectful tone ...*' Edsel raged, but Larna cut him short.

'We're telling the truth,' she said, using her reasonable voice again. 'We really don't know where the wand is. You can torture us to death and we still wouldn't be able to tell you.'

Edsel paused to think about this. He'd begun to feel slightly light-headed, his vision swimming, slightly in and out of focus. Scratching his neck vigorously, he dismissed the problem, putting it down to the after-effects of his epic battles with Edina and Tiblou. He paced around the hapless pair rubbing his chin like an absent-minded professor wrestling with some difficult philosophical problem, and then stopped in front of them.

Muttering to himself, he said, 'Don't know what's the matter with me! It's obvious what I need to do,' he paused, grinning evilly. 'Reverse the blocking spell and continue the questioning.' He raised his wand, bringing it down unnecessarily hard on both their heads. '**Rescindo retentia. Rescindo retentia.**' Immediately, both teenagers recalled burying Mordrog's wand in the tin box not far from Blithe Cottage back in their own era. Aron exchanged a knowing look with his sister, indicating they must now keep quiet at all costs. But it wasn't possible. Looking directly at Aron with a wicked grin on his face, Edsel told Flint to hold Larna tight by imprisoning her arms behind her back. Then he strode up to her, raised his arm and then paused to look at Aron.

'Are you watching, boy?' he shouted. Then he delivered a stinging blow with his open hand across Larna's face.

Her head jerked backwards causing her to see stars. She almost collapsed, but Flint prevented her from falling and prepared her for a second hit. He was laughing to himself, enjoying this immensely. Larna forced herself not to cry out. She was utterly determined not to show these odious stinking bullies that they were hurting her, but it was very hard - especially when Edsel backhand her another resounding crack onto the other side of her face. Her head jolted back again with the force of the blow.

'*Stop!*' Echoed round the silent valley, filling the sky with its pleading. But it wasn't Larna's voice that had uttered the cry. It was

Aron's. He couldn't cope with seeing his sister being beaten like this. It was worse, far worse, than being beaten up himself. He had to stop it at any cost.

'I'll tell you where the wand's hidden,' he whispered.

'I knew you would,' chuckled Edsel.

'It's...it's...' He gave Larna an apologetic look.

'Come on, boy, spit it The warlock was sure it was with excitement. Then, in a low voice as if wanting nobody to hear, Aron guiltily mumbled the secret that mattered so much to everybody, but Edsel didn't hear what he said.

'Don't whisper, I can't understand you. Speak up, will you?' demanded the Boggret, swaying from side to side with what appeared to be frustration and impatience.

But before Aron could speak again, a figure came charging out from behind the snow covered rocks and rugby-tackled the swaying Boggret, sending him sprawling on the ground in a groaning heap.

'Leave them alone!' shouted the furious newcomer. 'Don't you **dare** lay a finger on either of them again!'

Having missed Violet, he had decided to give up his search for the missing teenagers and look for his family instead. The trail Chet had followed had also led him through the Stone Forest to the Valley of Ice where he had spotted the group of figures in the distance. Racing up to them, he had just been in time to witness Larna's maltreatment before launching himself forwards to stop it. He scrambled up from the ground and embraced them both.

'Are you all right?' he asked anxiously.

Larna nodded, unable to speak because the blows to her face had made her cheeks and mouth swell up like balloons. A trickle of blood fell from a cut to her bottom lip where Edsel's long nails had caught her. Aron just nodded to confirm he was unhurt. Then they all looked round at Edsel who was lying on the ground, curled up like a baby, clutching his stomach and whimpering.

'What's wrong with him?' asked Chet in amazement. 'I didn't hit him that hard.'

'Be careful,' warned Aron. 'It's probably a trick.'

'Doesn't look like a trick to me,' commented Chet knowingly. 'He looks hurt, badly hurt.'

Then Aron remembered the poisoned dart Edina spat out and accurately find its target in Edsel's neck before she died. It had to be that! 'I think we're safe, Chet,' he said, explaining what had happened. 'I reckon Edsel may be dying, in agony by the look of things.'

'Ervs im ight,' spluttered Larna.

Aron agreed, 'Serves him bloody well right!'

'What about the other one?' asked Chet, looking all around. 'Thought I saw two ugly creatures when I arrived.'

'You're right!' exclaimed Aron. 'Where's Flint?'

They looked around in all directions, but failed to spot the younger Boggret making his way swiftly and silently between the frozen rocks with a smile of pure joy on his face.

CHAPTER TWENTY-SEVEN

CRYSTAL OF SOULS TAKES ONE MORE

The full blue moon had vanished and the sky was beginning to lighten suggesting fair weather for their journey back to Tiblou's. The first thing to do was reverse the cockroach spell. 'How do we do that?' asked Chet.

'Try and remember the spell that revokes Edsel's spell,' mumbled Larna. She'd been rubbing snow onto her face and the melting ice-cold water had reduced the swelling considerably, allowing her to talk more freely. But she still wasn't wasting any words.

'*We* don't know any magic!' cried Aron.

'Ssh! Thinking!' answered Larna, pacing round in a circle, fingers pressing her temples.

The other two watched and waited for a long time and were about to give up hope when she looked up eagerly and exclaimed, **'Rescindo!** That's the first part of the spell Edsel used to bring back our memory and all I can remember. And, it could work in this instance, what do *you* think, Aron?'

'Brilliant, sis,' he called. 'Now all we need is a wand and we're in business.'

Chet was happy to go along with whatever they suggested.

Larna pointed to Edsel's wand lying beside his prostrate form on the ground. The witch's poison dart had clearly fulfilled its deadly work and he remained completely motionless as Aron picked up the wand and held it gingerly in his hand as if he expected it to bite him at any moment. Overcoming his revulsion, he led the way over to the rock under which they'd seen everyone hide and waved the wand in a circle above it.

'RAVERTO,' he chanted. Nothing happened.

'Need other word,' muttered Larna, touching her sore lip. 'Word for cockroach'.

'I know that!' exclaimed Aron. 'We did some stuff about insects in Biology at school and I remember the proper name for them is 'blatt' something.'

'*Blattaria?*' queried Larna. 'I think I remember Edsel's spell now.'

So Aron tried again. This time he chanted, *'RAVERTO BLATTARIA!'* and the effect was instantaneous. The rock went dark, as if it and the surrounding area had been pulled into a black hole. With a suddenness that made the three jump, there was a series of blinding flashes as one by one the cockroaches were expelled from the middle of the blackness. Tibs came first followed by Annie, Zeb, June and finally Neve.

Chet's jaw dropped. 'Dad?' he cried. 'Oh Lord ... **Dad!'** He dashed towards his father and embraced him.

Zeb stepped back and inspected his eldest son. 'Chet, lad. You've grown up ...' Zeb wiped his eyes on the hair on the back of his hands. Both men laughed and hugged again.

Annie looked on shedding a tear.

Interrupting the emotional reunion, Larna asked anxiously, 'Where's Violet?'

'Here!' called a little voice as the final flash revealed the fairy hovering above the group once more, her delicate wings radiating joyous purple light.

'What happened to us?' asked Tibs, looking baffled and queasy.

'Why don't we tell you as we head for home?' suggested Aron. 'I don't know about you, but I've seen enough of this damn freezing place to last me a lifetime and I can't wait to see the back of it.'

'We need to do this first,' added Chet, taking Edsel's wand from Aron's hand and breaking it in half across his knee. Then he did the same with the two halves until the wand was reduced to a handful of fragments, like kindling wood, before he dropped them to the ground and stamped on them with his heel, grinding them almost to dust. 'That's better. Edsel's definitely a gonner and now so's his devil wand. He won't bother us anymore.'

The party was about to move off when Annie held up her hand.

'We can't do this,' she said.

'What do you mean, mum?' cried Tibs. 'It's all over. We've won the battle – just! Time to go home.'

Annie shook her head. 'I haven't got the strength for the journey back. Look at Neve. She can hardly stand. Poor Larna's black and blue and Aron isn't in great shape after the Swooper attack. None of us have had much sleep or food, except apples since yesterday. We need rest and sustenance, if we can find any before we can undertake a long trek again.'

'Where are we going to find that, my dear?' asked Zeb. 'This isn't exactly the most hospitable of places.'

'And I need to search for my wand. Edina took it and put it somewhere.'

'Follow me!' Annie hobbled over the ice bridge and entered Edina's castle, then went in search of the witch's food store.

There was plenty of room inside and they threw themselves down wearily on the nearest seats.

Annie called out, **'Neve,** you'll never believe what I think have found.'

Following Annie's voice into what appeared to be a trophy chamber, she gasped at the array of gruesome artefacts that Edina had on display. In pride of place was her wand.

The others gathered round also horrified at what they saw. There were Boggret heads and, many frozen parts of creatures that Larna and Aron did not recognize.

Grabbing her wand, Neve gave a hefty sigh of relief, her misty breath spiralled upwards towards the vaulted ceiling.

Clapping one hand over her mouth, the other on her stomach, Larna heaved and ran from the grisly chamber in disgust, the others followed suit.

Shivering with shock and cold, Larna said, 'We c-can't stay here,' her breath coming out like white clouds in the still air. She turned to her grandmother, 'Are **your** powers going to be strong enough to get us all back to Tiblou's now you have your wand?'

'I wish it was that simple, love. Tibs will have explained that the further we are from the Major Oak our wands lose some of its power. Sadly, even Tiblou's magic isn't that potent here, possibly just rudimentary spells and, our collective spells aren't strong enough to safely transport everyone back to Tibs'.'

Having done a quick recce, Annie bustled off again towards the staircase in one of the towers, beckoning June to follow her. She soon returned with a huge pile of sleeping rugs taken from the beds of Edina and the twins, just enough for one each. June appeared carrying a tray of bottles and jars taken from the kitchen area at one side. Some of the food in the containers looked highly suspicious, but nobody was in the mood to be fussy. They wolfed down everything in sight, their stomachs gurgling and bubbling with gratitude at it being something substantial after such a long fast.

Afterwards, everyone felt sleepy and settled down under their rugs, keeping close to one another for extra warmth. Chet stayed awake and kept guard. He was in the best shape of them all and had the strength to keep going. He sat in a high backed chair facing the front door, a rug wrapped round his legs. He remained there all night staring out into the inky blackness for any sign of trouble until his eye lids drooped and he fell asleep. Apart from an occasional distant cracking sound, like shattering glass, there was none. Nothing disturbed the sleepers.

Next morning, after another meal of Edina's unidentifiable food, everyone felt geared up and ready to go. Larna picked up her backpack and was going to sling it over her shoulder when she discovered it was dripping wet. She was about to mention it to the others when Tiblou appeared from the back of the building.

'Guess what I've found!' he chuckled, leading the others outside. He pointed to three brooms leaning against the glistening ice wall. Each one looked like medieval flat straw brooms with knotted wooden handles precariously held together with fraying twine. One was a conventional broom but, the other two had been re-jigged to resemble chopper bikes from the twentieth century. Most probably for the twins.

'What're they for?' Aron sniggered.

'You fly on them. Although, those two contraptions are a new take on a very old theme.' explained Neve.

'Look, I'll show you,' called Tibs, jumping onto the ordinary broom, it slowly rose into the air. Wobbling around, Tibs circled the group, navigating by holding the bristle ends of the broom. 'Pretty cool, eh?'

'It's a charming curiosity, dear,' commented Annie, dismissively. 'Not the time for playing around, though. I'd like to get away now we're rested and fed.'

'Hang on a minute, mum, I want to try something, see if it works.' said Tibs landing beside Annie. He took out his wand and cast a spell engulfing the brooms in white smoke. Nothing happened. So Violet helped and together they produced a series of further puffs that stretched away in a line along the wall. As the smoke cleared, there was a collective gasp. Even Tibs was amazed; his spell had duplicated the raggedy broomstick, plus handle bars, so there was a ride for everybody. They wouldn't have to walk home. They could fly!

Larna chose one of the brooms, 'Good magic certainly has its uses, even if it is filtered down,' she chuckled. 'Race you to the other end of the bridge,' she called, climbing on and promptly falling off.

The broom took off without her and soared high above the castle. A shrill whistle from Tiblou made the long handled brush shudder to a halt and point down. The view below showed that the rear high turrets of Edina's castle were beginning to melt and crumble.

There were some comic antics as the older members tried to fly their brooms, unaware that they were in danger of a different kind.

Annie jumped on one side and rolled off the other, falling frighteningly near the edge of the bridge and the chasm below, so did Chet, but neither were hurt as they landed in soft snow. Neve showed great mastery on hers having flown when she was young.

'I'm so pleased we have these,' Neve said, weaving in and out of some rocks, just for the pleasure of it, 'I still feel slightly disorientated and was dreading the long walk back. But this is going to be fun! Takes me back to my childhood.'

So it was a happy group who prepared to set off in a line from Edina's Ice Kingdom. They were oblivious of the fact that the castle was rapidly disintegrating and, the bridge was melting behind them and coming away from the castle wall.

The ground shuddered, the group teetered, and a loud crack like a gunshot echoed round the valley. A look of horror appeared on their faces.

Tiblou yelled, 'Mount your transport, run like hell, aim the handles upward and take off. *Don't* look back, and **don't** look down.'

A mad scramble resulted when the bridge began dropping into the chasm behind them as they ran. One by one they managed to take off. Except for Aron. His terrified screams echoed when the last lump of ice bridge broke away and he went hurtling down into the icy depths, along with his ride to safety.

Neve shrieked.

Tiblou plunged headfirst into the abyss and yelled, **'Grab my hand, Aron.'** As Aron tumbled perilously close to the bottom, Tiblou caught hold of one of Aron's flailing arms and, with the momentum of upward swing yanked him up on to the broom behind him. Eyes closed Aron held on to Tiblou for dear life.

'Stop wriggling or you'll have us both off.' Tiblou called over his shoulder to a terrified Aron.

They flew on until they exited the ice valley and landed just inside the forest of stone. Aron was still traumatized and as white as a ghost. His heart still racing, he couldn't stop trembling. Neve ran over and wrapped her arms round her grandson and guided him to sit on the nearest rock.

'You're safe now, Aron love, take slow deep breaths and calm down.' She crooned.

Violet eased herself out of Tiblou's top pocket, smoothed her shock of unruly hair, shook the creases out of her dress and wings and settled on a fossilized branch a little away from the group. She rested her chin in the palm of her hands and watched over them all. A smile of satisfaction creased her face. Edina was dead, her brats vanquished, Neve was safe, and the return of June and Zebedia was an added bonus. She sighed; the sun was shining and they would be back at Tiblou's in no time. All was right with the world.

* * *

Forward thinking as always, Annie had had the presence of mind to fill everyone's water bottles with melting snow so they all had cool water to drink on their journey. It proved a hot ride once they'd made their way into the gloomy forest, speeding above the rough bumpy track and weaving round the trees of stone. Still riding tandem, Aron's eyes were screwed shut as he continued to cling on to Tiblou.

As the camp where the remains of Chet's make-shift shelter came into view, Tiblou warned everyone to keep an eye out for Swoopers. This was their territory and there was no reason why they wouldn't attack again. But the skies remained empty and the danger was soon forgotten, except for the memory of that awful day when Ozzy's bravery had saved them. Annie, who was behind him at that point, noticed his head drop and flew alongside him with a reassuring smile.

'I'm sure Ozzy would be proud to know how he'd helped us to win this battle,' Annie said reassuringly.

'Yes, he would, Mum,' agreed Tibs sadly. 'He won't be forgotten.'

Annie nodded and dropped back in line. She knew he missed Ozzy very much and didn't believe he'd be happy with any other pet.

They flew on towards the shallow hill and, one by one they landed for a pit stop. Larna and Aron looked across to the outcrop of rock in the distance and exchanged silent glances. It held terrible memories for both of them now, of desolation and danger and the worst kind of slavery. For Larna it also held the memory of Cai, but she found her feelings had changed since she'd squeezed through that narrow gap and hurried down to the underworld in search of him. Her crush had faded. She acknowledged what she'd known all along and what he'd told her at their urgent parting was true. They were two completely different species from different worlds, centuries apart, and there was no way they could possibly be together. She was resigned to that now and it no longer saddened her. And that was liberating. She found her thoughts were now focused on what she was doing rather than always being somewhere else. And she was happy in other ways. Yaya was safe and there would no doubt be celebrations to enjoy before she returned to the peace of Blithe Cottage with her grandmother and brother.

The travellers were about to get underway again when a sudden wind sprang up. It howled across the empty plain like someone in pain, making everyone look at each other in alarm.

'It'll be hard to steer against this wind,' commented June, her fur rippling.

'Just take it slowly,' advised Violet, grabbing the collar of Tiblou's robe preventing herself from being blown away by another violent gust.

'I don't fancy setting off in this,' commented Neve, also finding it hard work. 'I think we should stay here for a while.'

'I think you should too,' said a croaking voice. A burst of flame shot upwards and Edsel crouched in front of them, doubled over with pain but alive.

'Surprised to see me again?' he whispered. 'You know me; I am your worst nightmare. Full of nasty surprises.'

It was clear the warlock was on his last legs, but he'd summoned up enough strength to find his enemies in order to take his final revenge.

'You can't harm us, Boggret,' scoffed Chet contemptuously. 'We smashed your wand to smithereens back there and that means you're powerless.'

'On the contrary,' Edsel wheezed, lifting his hand and pointing a shaky finger. 'You forget I have magic in my fingertips. I've one spell left and intend to use it. If it's the last thing I do, I'll take you all with me.'

Nobody knew what to do at this unexpected reversal of their fortunes and just stood there, gobsmacked, waiting for the end. But Larna could see he had only minutes to live and decided their only hope was to play for time. Bravely she stepped forward to confront the killer.

Neve said, 'No, Larna ... stay put.'

Larna twisted her head and whispered, 'I know what I'm doing.' then turned back to face Edsel. 'If you spare us I'll tell you where Mordrog's wand is hidden.' she said.

There was a loud gasp at this announcement, but Tiblou held up his hand to silence any protest. He realized what Larna was doing and knew how to help. Silently, closing his eyes and focusing his thoughts, he sent a telepathic message to the Grand High Council of witches and wizards for their help.

'What good would that do me now?' gasped Edsel, doubling right over as another wave of agonising pain coursed through his body.

'I just thought you might like to know,' replied Larna, not really knowing what to say next. 'You seemed pretty keen to get the information out of me back there at the bridge.

He looked up, his eyes glowing red with hatred and rage. 'That was then. This is now,' he groaned. 'I'll die happy if I think I'm taking you down with me and the world will be rid of your sickening goody-two-shoe ways.'

With that, he raised a trembling finger and tried to focus on firing it round the circle like a gun. But before he could loose off his dying spell, a glowing orb appeared in the distance and sped towards them like a glittering space ball. It knocked Edsel's finger aside, causing him to drop to the ground with a startled yell. The missile landed squarely in Tiblou's hand and opened. Larna and Aron recognised it straight away.

Inside, the crystal was primed for action as it had been before. Tibs raised the shimmering blue glass and uttered, *'ELLA CRYSTAL OF SOULS!* 'Glowing powerfully in the wizard's hand, it lifted Edsel off the ground and they watched him being sucked through the glass where he shrank to a minute size and swirled around inside the crystal like clothes inside a washing machine. His parting scream could be heard for miles around and everyone ducked as if a jet plane was flying low overhead, but it faded away as Edsel Banjax, the Boggret Warlock from Tophet, below Sherwood forest, disappeared forever; taking his place with the other tortured souls and polywigs who had given their lives to evil.

'Now we *are* safe,' sighed Neve with relief and great satisfaction. 'Let's go home.'

CHAPTER TWENTY-EIGHT

A WELCOME INTRUDER

Elva was out picking wild mushrooms for the evening meal in the Kitchen Cafe when she saw the line of figures on strange-looking flying machines approaching in the distance. Fearing this was some kind of new attack by the forces of evil; she scrambled to the nearest tree that was broad enough to hide behind. As soon as the flyers drew close enough for her to recognize the person at the front, she squealed with delight. Leaving her basket where it lay, she raced back to the café to tell Roger that the rescue party had returned.

Roger dashed outside as the procession arrived and saw them dismount and park their odd shaped brooms against the wall. Apart from the original one three they pop, pop, popped and disappeared. He laughed out loud in disbelief. 'Brush transpo now is it?'

'Better than that stagecoach death-trap,' commented Aron.

'What stagecoach?' Roger queried.

'Doesn't matter,' laughed Larna, casually waving her hand. 'It's all past history now.'

'*Well,* aren't you coming in ...?' asked Roger then he broke off as he spotted his sister June and Zebedia amongst the group. He stood rooted to the spot, unable to speak, in shock. Then he recovered and rushed over to embrace them in a warm bear hug that made Zeb laugh out loud, and nearly crushed June to death.

'Where have you **been?** What *happened?*' His tirade of excited questions went on and on until he began to run out of steam. 'I want to hear ... '

'We'll tell you the sordid story later.' Zeb cut in.

'As you wish.' Roger backed off, twitching his nose, '... Phew! you're whiffy, you both urgently need a shower.'

Stifling a laugh, Aron nudged his sister and whispered in her ear, 'and a haircut.'

'Come back later and we'll celebrate your safe return?' cried the café-owner, his eyes sparkling with the prospect. 'It's now five o'clock. Be here for eight.'

'Sounds good to me,' said Tibs, starting to make his way on foot. The others followed.

'We all need a good wash and a change of clothes,' Annie said as she kissed her brother on the cheek en passant.

'I couldn't agree more.' Added Neve, sniffing under her arms.

As they made their way through the trees, Aron looked back and noticed Elva standing behind the waving figure of Roger, watching him go. Seeing him turn, the girl raised her hand and gave a shy wave before disappearing round the back into the kitchen like a scalded cat. He gave a quick wave back, hoping Larna wouldn't notice. But she did and laughed at his beetroot-coloured face.

'You *are* smitten,' she said.

'Don't know what you're talking about,' he replied gruffly, looking away.

'You've got a crush on Elva and, by the look of things, she's got a crush on you.'

'Rubbish!'

Larna didn't comment. She just reached up and ruffled his hair, something he always hated.

'It's okay to have feelings, you know,' she relented.

'What, like you have for Cai?'

'That's not fair!'

'True though, isn't it?'

'No it's not, actually. Leastways, not anymore,' she said calmly, the conversation losing its bantering tone. 'I've given up that daydream, if you must know.'

Aron put an arm round her shoulders, 'Sorry, Lar. Couldn't have worked, you know.'

Neve looked on and smiled at the visible bond between her grandchildren.

By now they had almost reached their destination and found Tibs standing with one arm raised in warning. Neve and the teenagers hurried up to join Annie, Zeb and June who were already standing beside him. Chet, who was less tired and stressed, had stayed with Uncle Roger to help with the preparations and Violet had flown off to her own place until later.

'There's someone in the house,' the wizard whispered. 'I saw something move across one of the windows.'

'I can't see anything,' said June.

'Me, neither,' agreed Zeb.

So they waited and watched and, sure enough, there was a faint sound from inside followed by a flash of grey.'

'I saw something then!' cried Larna.

'I did too, I think,' said Aron.

'Who do you think it could be?' A worried frown creased Tiblou's face. 'We've eliminated all our known enemies ... haven't we?'

'Oh for goodness sake, stop faffing about.' scoffed Annie, pushing everyone aside and marching boldly up to the front door. She rapped on it loudly with her knuckles.

'OZZY!' she shouted. 'Come on out! We're back.'

There was a long pause and the others were beginning to dread Annie had made a terrible mistake when a big fluffy shape squeezed itself through the flap at the side of the building and hurtled towards them, squawking delightedly. Ozzy made straight for Tibs and knocked him over with his puppy-like frenzy of excitement at seeing his master again. Although Tibs landed in a flowerbed, his already scruffy garment added another layer of grime and soil, but he didn't mind one bit and rolled over and over on the ground hugging the bird and laughing.

Once Zebedia had got over his disbelief of a tame Swooper, in a stronger voice he said. 'Good God, I think they're pleased to see each other.'

Everyone laughed except Annie who waited until the joyful reunion was over before looking down and wagging one finger in the Swooper's face.

'You're twice the size you were before we left,' she scolded. 'Have you been scoffing all the food in my larder?'

Ozzy gave an apologetic squawk and hung his head. He couldn't have looked guiltier if he'd tried. Suddenly, Annie burst out laughing and bent down to embrace him.

'You're very naughty ... but I forgive you.'

It wasn't possible to find out how Ozzy had fared when the wild Swoopers discovered they'd been tricked by his false alarm-call, or how he'd managed to escape their wrath. But it didn't matter. All that anybody cared about was that the bird had managed to return home unscathed and was waiting for them. Tibs was particularly elated because he'd really believed his pet had been killed and he wouldn't see him again. To find him alive and well – a bit too well, if truth be told – was a fantastic bonus.

'We've come through a lot these last few days and everything's gone well in the end, but this is the icing on the cake,' he chuckled.

'Speaking of icing on the cake,' said Annie, looking at her timepiece. 'It's time we went inside if we're going to get ready for

Roger's party. We've a great deal to do in the next three hours.'

Tired, dirty and dishevelled as they all were, nobody wanted to get washed and changed until the important business had been completed. So Tibs led everyone into the sitting room and invited them to sit on the chairs to watch.

'Watch what?' Aron asked his sister.

'Don't you remember anything?' groaned his sister. 'Zeb and June's conversion back to full human beings, of course.'

'Oh, yeah!' said Aron, grinning. 'Beats shaving any day.'

An expectant hush fell over the room as the wizard opened a locked cupboard with a set of keys he produced by clicking his fingers three times.

'These keys are kept hidden by being invisible ...' he began to explain.

'No need for chapter and verse, Tibs dear,' Annie was impatient. 'Please just get on with it. We trust you completely. Your father here can't wait another minute for the miracle conversion.'

Larna noticed that it was the ancient book with the hollowed out middle which contained two vials.

Tibs opened up the book, released a vial out of the tiny hands which held it securely in the soft-lined case in which it was stored, he held it up to the light and shook it. Gazing at it for a long time, he nodded his head in satisfaction and turned to the others.

'This special spell needs a rhyme, if you remember. I'll say it first, then I'd be grateful if you'd all repeat it together.' He cleared his throat.

> **'Hear ye, hear ye,**
> **Change all back to what they should be**
> **After years of sorrow and pain**
> **June and Zeb shall be whole again!'**

When this had been recited a second time, Tiblou took the cork stopper out of the special phial and a rainbow of DNA strands shot into the air. They spiralled round and round, as if looking for their targets, and then headed down towards Zeb and June. The couple had been advised to put their head back, tongues out and the delicate helixes would dissolve on impact. The effect was instant and astonishing. Their animal features, long ears, tails and body hair they had endured for so long began to disappear, their frames more upright until they became fully human beings again. The filthy rags

149

they were wearing hung on their new human bodies.

'With the DNA spirals we produced after Larna and Aron kindly donated some of their Gorry blood, on their first visit, we were able to reverse the mutation curse...'

As Tiblou put the phial carefully back in its box and magicked away the secret keys, Zeb and June did a dance of joy.

'Well done Tiblou, Balgaire would be very proud of you, as am I.' Neve said.

'Save your energy, you two,' Annie told them. 'There'll be plenty of dancing at the party later.'

'Will there, Larna?' whispered Aron, looking at his sister with a horrified expression. 'No way, I'm not dancing.'

'You'll be all right,' she soothed.

'I won't!' he insisted with great feeling. 'I'll make a fool of myself and that will be a disaster!'

There was no time to worry about this further because Neve ushered the pair of them upstairs for a shower. And attend to her own ablutions.

'There are clean towels on the rail and plenty of soap in the dish,' she told them. 'Don't forget to wash behind your ears.'

'You're back to your old self again, Yaya,' said Larna, giving her grandmother an affectionate hug.

'That's right,' Neve chuckled. 'So you two better watch your step from now on.'

'What are we supposed to do for clothes?' asked Aron, indicating his torn jeans and filthy, blood stained t-shirt. 'We can't go to the party looking like this.'

'I think Tibs said he'd sort something out for you,' called Neve.

In fact, the wizard was waiting for them on the landing outside their rooms.

'Stand still please,' he said. 'This won't take a second.' Then he flicked his wand towards them, just touching their clothes lightly, and they both found brand new carbon copies of the things they were wearing folded over his other arm.

'Thanks,' they gasped together.

'Completely clean and guaranteed to fit perfectly,' he chuckled. 'Enjoy your showers.'

With mock fury, they shoved Tibs away down the corridor and slammed their bathroom doors behind them.

CHAPTER TWENTY-NINE

A TIME OF CELEBRATION

As a special treat and reward for his outstanding bravery, Ozzy was allowed to go to the party too. Annie wasn't keen on the idea at first.

'He'll get over-excited and make a lot of noise,' she warned. 'And he'll probably eat all the food. Look at him – he looks like a barrel already.'

Ozzy hung his head in his usual sad manner, pleading with his eyes to be given what he wanted, and Tiblou did the same! He said nothing, matching his pet's pathetic expression and imploring look. He looked so funny and so ridiculous that Annie couldn't help but laugh.

'Oh all right then,' she relented. 'But promise to be on your best behaviour – both of you!'

Ozzy raced round the room in a feathered frenzy of joy, breaking all the rules already.

This was the moment Larna and Aron chose to return to the sitting room after their showers.

'Whatever's going on?' gasped Larna, laughing at the crazy antics going on in front of them.

'It's Ozzy, dear,' explained Annie. 'He's leading my son astray.'

Larna and Aron laughed until they cried.

'It was worth coming here just for this,' spluttered Aron.

* * *

The guests arrived at Roger's café a little after eight. Annie had delayed them which gave Chet time to dash to Tibs for a quick clean-up and change of clothes.

Ozzy was trying to behave himself, but the excitement of being allowed to be with everyone on such an important occasion kept getting the better of him. He couldn't sit still on Tiblou's arm and when the wizard walked up to the entrance the bird was trying to balance on his head. They expected Ozzy to be crazy and this was a night of fun and celebration, so a bit of craziness was perfectly acceptable.

Annie was sitting at a table with Neve, Zeb and June as Violet flew in through the window to complete the guest-list. She was wearing a plain pink outfit, which puzzled everybody, until she started changing the colour of her wings as she went round greeting her friends. One minute she was a glowing green, next moment dazzling red, then deep orange, shining purple, sky blue...and so on, like a living rainbow. Everyone stopped and clapped her, marvelling at the beauty of her appearance.

'Thank you,' she said, turning a breathtaking shade of her natural purple, 'glad you like it.'

Larna noticed Aron looking round for Elva, but she was very busy in the kitchen helping Chet and Roger to prepare the party food.

'I'm sure she'll be out later,' Larna said with a smile.

'Doesn't bother me,' replied Aron, shrugging his shoulders.

In fact, Elva appeared a few moments later, carrying out some special-looking jugs which she placed on a long table in the corner. The jugs had tiny wings on the side.

'Ladies and gentlemen,' called Roger, clapping his hands to gain everyone's attention. 'I'd like to propose a toast to the safe return of all our friends, the ***miraculous*** appearance of Zeb and June and the banishment of evil from Upper Sherwood. So please raise your glasses with me...***To June and Zebedia.*** '

'There's nothing in them, Roger!' called Tiblou.

'Wait for it, dear,' commented Annie. 'It's another one of Balgaire's legacies to my brother. He gifted Roger and this Kitchen Café with a few spells making chores easier for him.' She paused for breath. 'He was also instrumental for the magic mugs. In addition to the waiter-less plates they'd seen last time and the self-erecting decorations that now adorned the room, her brother had invented a new system for serving drinks. At his command, the flying jugs took off into the air and swooped round the room, pouring a delicious green liquid into everyone's glasses. The jugs all performed perfectly except for one which appeared to have a faulty wing. This one flew round and round in circles before tipping out its contents and crashing to the ground. Unfortunately, Chet happened to be directly underneath it and the deluge of drink went all over his head.

'I'm ***so*** sorry,' cried Roger, grabbing a tea towel and rushing over to dab Chet dry. 'Still needs perfecting.' But the big man didn't mind at all. He burst out laughing and so did the others, holding onto each other with mirth as they looked at his plastered-down hair and green-coloured face.

'Great here, isn't it?' grinned Aron.

His evening got even better when Roger started the music. There was nothing miraculous about this – he just switched on the juke box that formed the centre of his Fifties-style diner. And when it first began, Aron's spirits dropped. This was the moment he'd been dreading. As everyone else took to the floor and began moving together in time to the music, he felt lost. The new Zeb and Annie danced together. Chet took Larna's hand. June and Tibs were partners. Aron was left on his own, partner less and not knowing what to do next. Then Elva appeared. Her chores completed, she left the kitchen and came to join the party. Seeing Aron on his own, her face lit up with a pretty smile and, overcoming her previous shyness, she walked right over to him. Saying nothing, she held out her hand, inviting him onto the floor. At first he shook his head, but Elva wasn't taking no for an answer and continued to hold out her hand until he accepted it. And then the evening was magic. The music changed to rock 'n' roll and everyone began jiving. Aron found that by copying his new partner and letting himself respond to the rhythm of the music, he could do quite well. Soon he was swirling Elva round by the hand and pulling her to and fro like the others, joining in the laughter and excitement. It was the highlight of Aron's holiday, something he would remember for months to come when the memory of all the dangers and terrors were beginning to fade.

'I've never seen Aron so happy!' Larna shouted to Neve. She was pleased for her brother, really pleased, but a brief wave of sadness passed over her face as she realized she was the loser in love here and he was the winner.

The climax of the evening came when the dancing was over and everyone sat down exhausted. Lots of delicious food was served by the flying waiter plates and then Roger pulled some decorative curtains aside to reveal the biggest cake anyone had ever seen. It had layers of chocolate and orange sponge with sections of thick cream in-between and a topping of pink icing with a gigantic cherry in the middle.

'Does it explode like your fantastic ice-cream?' called Aron.

'Wait and see,' chuckled Roger, placing some small empty plates in a circle round the giant gateau. 'But you're not far off.'

'If this is gonna do what I think it's gonna, I'm taking cover!' announced Chet.

'You don't need to worry,' replied Roger, waiting for more

laughter to finish. 'This one's been thoroughly tried and tested.'

Pausing for a moment, keeping everyone in suspense, Roger suddenly clapped his hands and the cake collapsed like a building that's been blown up and demolished. Everyone gave a joint gasp of horror until they saw the cake had divided itself into neat slices of different sizes that were dropping onto the plates as they passed by on their own. Then the plates flew over to the guests and circled round slowly like the dishes on offer in a sushi bar. Everyone pointed to the slice of their choice and the plate duly landed in front of them. Chet chose the biggest one so Aron, not to be outdone, chose two and ate them both with the speed of light.

'This collapsing cake tastes *delicious!*' he murmured.

'Glad you like it,' chuckled Roger, beaming with delight. 'Have you got room for a third slice?'

Leaving Aron chatting happily with Elva and the others laughing at Ozzy who'd been allowed to have a small piece of cake as well and had got it all over himself like a toddler, Larna got up and went outside for a breath of air. She was enjoying the cool and the silence when she found Tiblou beside her.

'Great minds and all that,' he said, standing beside her. They watched the moon and stars shining down on them through the dome that covered this world for a long peaceful time. Then Tibs gave a sigh.

'Something wrong?' asked Larna.

'I'm not sure,' Tiblou answered.

Larna turned to face the young wizard. 'Go on, tell me,' she urged.

'Well it's probably nothing,' he said with another anxious sigh, 'I just have the feeling something still isn't right.'

'What do you mean?'

'I don't know. We're all here having a wonderful time together, but something's niggling at the back of my mind makes me feel it isn't over yet. The battle's still not won. I don't know why I feel like this, but I just do. It feels like a... like a premonition.'

'Maybe, after all we've been through – especially you; maybe you're worried that if you relax something else might go wrong.'

'You could be right, Larna,' agreed Tibs, turning to her with a wry smile. 'No doubt time will tell.' But as they turned to re-join the party, Larna going in through the door ahead of him, he added to himself...

'But somehow I don't think so.'

CHAPTER THIRTY

FORCE OF EVIL

Neve had almost completely recovered from her horrifying ordeal and was eager to get home. 'I want to see the damage you tell me Edina did to the cottage when she kidnapped me,' she told Larna and Aron at breakfast next morning. 'I hate mess. I want to get everything straight again as soon as we get home.'

Larna didn't want much to eat. Uncle Roger's collapsing cake had proved very filling and, besides, she was anxious about Tiblou's words last night. Supposing his hunch was right and a new threat hung over Sherwood? The prospect didn't bear thinking about when they'd only just got rid of the previous one. So she pushed the matter out of her mind and nibbled at her piece of toast. Aron, on the other hand, tucked into a huge bowl of porridge with milk and brown sugar and then held it out for more like Oliver Twist. He knew nothing of the wizard's forebodings and no amount of rich food the night before could blunt his appetite next day.

The visitors were just finishing their breakfast when the door crashed open and in came Ozzy. He didn't fly because he wasn't allowed to inside the house, so he waddled as fast as he could be looking like a big grey feathery penguin. He jumped up onto Larna's lap and pecked her nose.

'*Ouch!*' she wailed. 'That hurt!'

'He's only being friendly and giving you a loving greeting,' said Aron. 'Don't be such a wuss.'

But then the bird leaped onto Aron's lap and pecked him even harder.

'*Get off, pest!*' he shouted, rubbing his throbbing nose.

'Who's the wuss now?' sniggered Larna.

'Is Ozzy misbehaving again?' asked Tiblou, hearing the commotion and coming into the room to see what was going on.

'No it's okay, Tibs,' answered Larna. 'Aron says Ozzy's just being affectionate.'

Ozzy was banished to the corner where he sat with his head forward on the ground in his submissive pose. But he was just biding his time. As soon as the others left the room, he was up on the table gobbling up all the left-over food.

Annie discovered the mess when she came in to clear the dishes and chased him outside squawking, in a flurry of feathers. Meanwhile, Larna and Aron were instructed to be ready to leave and be by the front door in ten minutes. He was accompanying Neve and her grandchildren back to past Sherwood.

'I have to give Clem the Crystal of Souls,' he'd explained.

As Larna and Aron joined Neve under the beautiful drooping tree, they found everyone waiting to bid them goodbye. So they went along the line together, like players at the start of a football match. Zeb and June were first. They were almost unrecognisable without their fur and with shoes on their feet.

'We can never thank you enough for rescuing us from that life of hell,' said Annie's husband, kissing Larna on both cheeks and shaking Aron warmly by the hand. June did the same.

'Wonder how those dreadful twins are getting on in our place,' she chuckled. 'I can't imagine they'll take kindly to cooking food they're never allowed to eat and washing pots all day long.'

Annie came next, not saying anything. Tearing up, she just held out her arms to both the teenagers and enfolded them in a warm embrace as if they were her own offspring.

'We think you were very brave, Annie,' whispered Larna.

'Nonsense!' She scoffed. 'You were the brave ones. *And* the foolish ones! Don't you ever wander off on your own again, either of you. Do you hear?' She laughed and looked years younger.

'Yes, Annie,' grinned Aron.

Chet shook both their hands, nearly crushing their fingers to pulp. 'See you both again very soon, I hope,' he said.

'We hope so too,' smiled Larna.

'Where's Violet?' asked Aron, looking all round.

'Here!' called the fairy, swooping down from a ledge where she'd been sitting and watching the departure.

'You looked stunning last night, Violet,' called Larna.

'What about this morning?' Violet was wearing a crimson outfit and her wings were shining with variated mauve, purple and indigo.

'You look even more stunning today,' added Aron quickly. He was ever wary of the fairy's quick temper and didn't want anything to upset her in these precious final moments.

'Come on,' called Neve, starting to depart with Tibs and beckoning her grandkids to follow. 'That's enough fond farewells. The daily downpour is due soon and we need to reach the time portal if we're to avoid another soaking. The instant drying machine hasn't been invented yet in our time.'

Larna hurried off as she'd been told, but Aron hung back as if he still had unfinished business.

'She's just coming,' Annie told him, pointing into the distance with a smile. Elva was hurrying through the trees with Roger puffing along behind her. They stopped to say their goodbyes to the others and then arrived at Tiblou's.

'Farewell, old chap,' boomed Roger, clapping Aron on the back as if the boy was choking and he was trying to dislodge something from his throat. 'Wonderful to see you again and glad you liked the catering. I'll come up with something else even more exciting next time.'

'I'll look forward to that,' mumbled Aron, regaining his pose. Then Elva came over and stood in front of him. Like at their first meeting, they didn't know what to say and just stood there looking at each other awkwardly. But Elva had made the first move at the dance last night, so Aron felt it was his turn now. He leaned forwards and kissed her gently on the cheek. Then blushing with embarrassment, he ran off to join his sister and the others without another backward glance. Elva stood holding her cheek and smiling.

'You'll see him again, Elva,' said Uncle Roger kindly, putting his arm round her shoulder. 'They'll be back before long, I'm sure of it.'

The trek to the portal was short and uneventful. There were no hostile eyes watching from the bushes or deadly attacks coming out of the blue. With the double threat of Edina and Edsel having cancelled each other out, Upper Sherwood felt a peaceful place for the first time in ages. The only people the foursome encountered were Roger's customers, the locals who smiled and waved and called their thanks yet again for being freed of their animal mutations. Clementine was waiting for them on this side of the divide. Her flame red hair an untidy mass.

'I've told my brother you're coming, Master Tiblou,' she said. 'He's expecting you.'

'Thank you.' replied the smiling wizard.

'Goodbye again, you two,' she said, putting her wizened hands on their shoulders. 'Your visits are always … eventful?' And for the first time her face cracked a smile.

'It wasn't all down to us, Clementine,' said Larna modestly.

'Are you *really* from the Middle Ages and was a friend of Robin

Hood?' Aron blurted out.

'I am, and was,' chuckled Clementine, 'but there's no time to tell you about it now. You must get back to your own time. Your grandmother's impatient to be home.'

Aron looked across at Neve who was waiting with an expression of forced patience on her face.

The magic rituals were chanted *'ELLA VITA'* three times. Within seconds the monolith rose and Larna and Aron were pulled backwards through time to find themselves in their own century, on the other side of the portal. Tiblou had travelled with Neve a split second before and was waiting for them.

'Where's Clem?' asked Neve, looking all around.

'Here!' he called, flapping down from an overhanging branch in crow form and morphing into human shape as his feet touched the ground. 'I never stray very far from my post, don't ya know.'

Tibs reached inside his robe and brought out the Crystal of Souls, tossing it across to Clem.

'Careful!' the old man cried in alarm. 'You'll break it.'

'No chance of that,' chuckled Tibs. 'I put a preserving spell on it as soon as it swallowed up Edsel. You couldn't break it if you tried.'

'I see the evil creature's been banished forever,' holding up the crystal and looking right through it so his eye looked distorted by the liquid inside. 'Best place for the lot of 'em.' Clem said, scratching his head with the bony fingers of his right hand, his cap clutched in his left.

It was a cool clear day in modern Sherwood, one of those days that give the first hint autumn is just around the corner even though it's still high summer. Larna and Aron enjoyed walking through the ancient trees, proud to be with Tibs, relieved to be with Neve and excited to be back home. They found Blithe Cottage as they had left it with all the debris of Edina's explosive visit scattered in every room.

'I was hoping the fairies might have been in and tidied up a bit,' laughed Larna.

'There are no such things as fairies, child,' Neve joked back. 'I don't know, believing in the supernatural at your age!' She winked.

With Tiblou's help, the rooms were soon cleared up and everything put back in its place. The damage wasn't as bad as it had looked, just a few broken vases and picture frames that Neve didn't mind about and the grandfather clock that she passionately did.

'I can fix this for you,' said Tibs, opening the door in the front and touching the buckled coils and springs with his wand. Instantly they righted themselves. The pendulum moved slowly from side to side and the clock started ticking again before sounding the hour in its usual mellow booming tones.

'Time for tea,' chucked Neve.

As Neve sat with Aron and Tiblou, relishing the warming cuppa she'd yearned for so long, Larna got up and wandered outside, saying she wanted a spot of sunshine. She made her way down to the gate and stood with her head on one side, listening intently. There was no sound other than the singing of the birds in the trees and the distant hum of traffic as other holidaymakers came to visit the forest. Larna was terrified she'd hear the knocking noise again, the sound that meant Mordrog's wand was still looking for a new master. But this wasn't the case. It must have been doing it before, sensing Edina was nearby. Now she was gone, it was silent. Smiling to herself, she turned back towards the cottage with a smile.

'All's well that ends well,' she said to herself.

* * *

The plan was to retrieve Mordrog's wand so Tibs could destroy it and return to future Sherwood before nightfall. But, the white witch leaned forward with her arms on the kitchen table and began massaging her temples.

'You feeling alright, Yaya?' enquired Larna.

'I'm afraid I'm not,' Neve sighed. 'I've another of my headaches coming on. I think I'm winding down after a long period of extreme cold and stress and, the moment I relax that's me finished for the rest of the day. I'm not as young as I once was. I'll have an early night, be as right as rain tomorrow morning.'

'That's fine, Neve,' said Tiblou with a smile. 'I had meant to return to *my* time zone before sunset but ... oh well, there's no real hurry to get back. There's no danger now, so I'm not needed. You go and rest. We can amuse ourselves, Mordrog's wand buried for a few more hours can't do any harm. After all, it's been there for long enough.'

So Neve retired to her room where the notice panel outside the door amended itself to ***Please call at 6.30am for early start*** and soon the sound of gentle snoring could be heard from upstairs. Larna and Aron fetched out a board game and invited Tibs to join them. They soon found he was winning because he used words from his magic vocabulary like Mensa and Veritas.

'We don't know whether they're real words or not,' complained Aron.

'You'll just have to trust me then, won't you?' grinned the wizard.

'Two can play at that game,' whispered Larna, winking at her brother. So she invented the name Pollywig.

'What does that mean?' asked Tiblou.

Struggling to keep a straight face Larna explained, 'It's a rare type of dolphin that has evolved to swim in icy waters. They're found at both the North and South Poles.'

'Okay, I'll let you win this one,' said Tibs with a sigh.

Now it was Aron's turn. He went one step further by making up words that used all the high-scoring letters like ZAXQ and VUQUZ.

'Definitions, please,' demanded their opponent.

'Well,' said Aron, stalling for time while his brain went into overdrive, 'ZAXQ is a type of spear used by ancient African warriors and VUQUZ is a drink made from sweet yams in South America ...'

Up until this point, Tibs believed him but, unlike his sister, Aron was unable to maintain the bluff and started smirking before he could finish.

'Oh, you dirty rotten cheats!' he cried, knocking the board over with his hand. Then they all laughed so loudly they feared they would wake up Neve.

Addressing Larna, Tibs gleefully informed her, 'Gotchya though. In my world Pollywig is a real word, and it isn't a dolphin, though it does swim for a while. So you weren't cheating me after all.'

The three of them retired to bed after that, agreeing an early night would be welcome as they also felt jaded after the ordeals of recent days.

Their beds felt heavenly after so many nights sleeping rough and they were all soon peacefully drifting off. But, around midnight, a thunderstorm shook the cottage. A series of lightning flashes illuminated the rooms followed by deafening claps of thunder. Aron slept through it, of course, and so did Neve whose medication had zonked her out. But Larna sat bolt upright in bed, puzzling at the violent storm which hadn't been forecast and was completely unexpected. Tibs stood at his window, looking out at the dramatic flashes of lightning and lashing rain, his sense of foreboding growing deeper with every flash and crash.

Then Larna heard laughter. It echoed round her room, growing louder and louder, until she had to clap hands over her ears and yell, *'Stop!'* The laughter continued to surround her until, mercifully, it began to fade away very slowly and then disappeared. Larna was reminded of the visitations she'd had from Edina at the start of this holiday and knew this laughter boded ill. She jumped out of bed, threw on her clothes and went to find Tiblou.

The wizard had heard the laughter too and was equally alarmed.

'We need to retrieve the wand immediately,' he said with a grim expression.

'I'll wake Aron,' Larna called, making for the door.

'Does he need to come?' asked Tibs.

'He'd never forgive us if we left him out of this,' answered Larna. 'But Yaya's all right. Best leave her where she is.'

Aron was most indignant at being woken up in the middle of a dream about Elva and annoyed at the idea of going to find the wand.

'It's the middle of the night,' he protested, 'and it's pouring with rain!'

'Doesn't matter,' hissed Larna, pulling his arm impatiently. 'This is important. Now get a move on, will you?'

Five minutes later, dressed in their waterproofs and wellington boots, the teenagers strode out into the continuing storm.

'What about you, Tibs?' asked Larna, 'You'll get soaked.'

'I'm fine, thanks,' he answered.

'Course he is,' Aron added. 'He can dry himself off instantly with that whizzy magic of his. Don't you remember anything, divit?'

'I'm *not* a divit.'

'That's enough,' Tiblou interrupted irritably. 'Now is not the time for squabbles.

Both Larna and Aron knew the way to the spot where the wand was buried and found it easily even though it was dark and the pelting rain made visibility poor. As they neared the place, they heard a repeated sound. Different from the knocking of the wand inside the tin. It sounded more musical than that, a hollow note like someone playing a steel drum. Dread flooded through Larna, making her feel sick, as she realized what it was. It was the sound of heavy rain on the metal tin. It wasn't buried anymore! It was out in the open!

Stopping dead in her tracks, the girl's worst fears were realized. There was the tin, lying open on the ground beside the hole, and it was empty. Larna, Aron and Tiblou all looked at each other, speechless with disbelief and horror.

'Who the...?' muttered Aron at last.

'Does it matter?' sighed Tibs. 'It's gone, that's what matters. We're too late!'

'I dread telling Yaya,' murmured Larna near to tears.

'So do I,' said Tibs.

* * * *

Neve was surprisingly calm when they broke the news to her next morning.

'This is my fault,' she said wearily. 'If I hadn't had a headache we would have found that cursed wand before it was taken.'

'That's silly,' said Aron, putting a soothing hand on his grandmother's arm. 'You couldn't help it.'

'Aron's right,' agreed Tibs, 'and what's done is done. That's a phrase you're very fond of yourself, Neve.'

The witch gave a wan smile. 'So who do you think took it?' she asked.

'We have no idea, Gran,' said Larna. 'We debated that question all the way back and long into the night, but none of us have any idea.'

'It's imperative that I go forward to my time and ....'

Just then, there was a loud tap on the kitchen window. Looking up, they saw Clem perched on the windowsill clearly anxious to get in. Neve jumped up to open it and the crow flew in, morphing into human shape in the middle of the floor.

'I have something to report, don't ya know,' he said, looking serious.

'Go on, Clem.' invited Tiblou. 'Give us the worst.'

'Last night, during the height of the storm, I thought I heard noises coming from the portal. But I put it down to the deafening thunder and failed to investigate further. I've neglected my duties, I'm afraid.' Clem hung his head.

'You haven't done that for a thousand years,' Neve told him. 'Now get on with it, man, what's happened?'

Clem looked up again. 'This morning,' he continued, 'when I went to check on the portal, I found it had been forced. Someone has got their hands on a key; how they managed that I really don't know – the whole mechanism was above ground and, the monolith has vanished. There were marks on the grass indicating someone had been through and then transported back again.'

As an afterthought he said, 'Oh, and there was a nasty smell lingering in the air.'

The others looked baffled by Clem's news, except for Aron. 'Oh my God,' he whispered, 'I know who it is.

* * * *

A few weeks later, at the beginning of September, two shadowy figures could be seen meeting up outside 23 ½ Vulcan Mews. It was approaching eleven o'clock at night and the younger of the two looked tired.

'Go home and get some sleep, Jonty,' advised Mr Waight. 'You've got extracurricular studies tomorrow, and, we have to keep up appearances.'

'You need to rest as well, sir,' said Jonty.

'I can make do with very little sleep, but you can't. You're a growing lad.' the man answered. 'So do as I say, please.'

'Nothing to report, anyway,' said Jonty, starting to depart. He stopped and looked back. 'Do you really think Flint the Boggret now has Mordrog's wand and is hell bent on eliminating the Gorrys? And intends to dominate future Sherwood?'

'I've no doubt about it, lad,' answered the teacher, his face lined with worry. 'Tiblou messaged me that Aron remembers seeing Flint's reaction out of the corner of his eye when he revealed where Mordrog's wand was buried. Now the villain believes he has assumed the mantle of a mighty Boggret warlock. Aron and Larna still need our protection, so, go home and sleep. Sherwood is as much at risk as it was before. So, the fight goes on ....'

To the bitter end.